Contents

OXFORD
UNIVERSITY PRESS

Chapter One:

Aunty Jum Jum
comes to Tea

It was difficult enough being twelve, thought Saif in annoyance as he slammed his bedroom door shut, 'without his mother forcing him to meet smelly old relatives who pinched his cheeks and left wet, sloppy kisses all over his face.

The very thought of a wet cheek made Saif shudder. He tossed himself onto his bed and sighed. Aunty Jum Jum was coming to tea. She was the worst of his mother's distant relatives, always hugging him into her musty shalwar kameez so tightly that he couldn't breathe!

One time, when she waddled over to say hello, Taimur, Saif's twin brother, panicked and pushed Saif towards her. All Saif saw was a brief glimpse of the gigantic hairy mole on Aunty Jum Jum's chin before he was hugged so hard that he wheezed and choked on the smell of her Amla hair oil!

Then Aunty Jum Jum turned her large, tank-shaped body towards Taimur. Taimur was hauled even further into Aunty Jum Jum's arms, and Saif could swear he heard a little shriek from his brother before he disappeared entirely.

'Little darlings,' Aunty Jum Jum gushed, squeezing with all her might.

Saif groaned. And now they had to have tea with her and be polite! It wouldn't be so bad if school was still open and he could make the excuse that he had homework to do, but school was out for the summer and Mama was already complaining that he and Taimur spent too much of their time watching movies and playing computer games.

That afternoon, the twins had promised to play football with Safi, Wali, Zara, and Alina, their good friends. Saif had even ironed his brand new Chelsea T-shirt, especially for the occasion! But now, thanks to Aunty Jum Jum's visit, the match would have to be postponed. Saif sighed. Safi and Wali were leaving for London in a week and he and Taimur wouldn't see them for two whole months! It wasn't fair.

From outside the bedroom door, Saif heard somebody start to wail. He watched as Taimur burst into the room, a look of terror on his face. Yup. Taimur must have heard the news. 'It's her! She's coming! For tea!' Taimur was breathless, and more than slightly panicked.

'Yeah, well,' grumbled Saif. 'We still have sometime before five, maybe we can think of a good excuse to stay in our room.'

'You know Mama's not going to let us get away with that!' replied Taimur. 'And this is your fault!'

'Me?' Saif protested, getting up from his bed. 'What do I have to do with anything?'

'It's because of how we tried to get out of tea last time. You remember? It was your stupid idea! Now nothing we say to Mama is going to work.'

Saif winced. A month earlier, when Aunty Jum Jum was due for a visit, he'd had the wonderful idea of pretending that the twins had measles so they wouldn't have to see her. He managed to convince Taimur to go along with the plan. They borrowed Mama's lipstick to put little red dots all over their faces. Mama didn't fall for it and was not amused.

'I'm not listening to anymore of your stupid schemes,' Taimur grumbled to his brother. 'Let's enjoy what time we have left of the afternoon, and do something fun to make us forget about Aunty Jum Jum.'

'As if we ever could.' Saif was only grateful that mother didn't usually see Aunty Jum Jum more than once a month. She was the cousin of their mother's second cousin, and yet insisted that they were her closest family! The twins knew that Mama felt sorry for Aunty Jum Jum, who had no

OXFORD
UNIVERSITY PRESS

immediate family of her own and spent much of her time travelling between relatives.

'Maybe if she stopped talking for two minutes, her relatives would invite her to stay for longer amounts of time,' suggested Baba, when he was in a mischievous mood. But Mama would just shoot Baba a look of irritation, and point out that Aunty Jum Jum had a good heart. Both Saif and Taimur were firmly on Baba's side in the matter.

'I know,' suggested Taimur. 'Let's have a look at that book Fooey Mamoo got us on haunted places in Pakistan. It looked really interesting, and I never got to finish it—you hogged it all of yesterday. That should put us in a good mood!'

Saif nodded, and pulled the book out from his shelf.

Even though they were twins, Saif and Taimur were very different. Saif loved arts and crafts, while Taimur loved electrical and mechanical things. Saif liked to go on *shikar* and shoot wild animals, while Taimur had a passion for dogs.

But there was a passion; one interest, that they shared in common. It was a unique, extremely exciting passion. It was a passion for ghost hunting!

It all started when they were young, and Nina Nana, their Great-aunt, filled their heads with stories of ghouls that used to haunt her house in Bahawalpur. Then their grandmother, Nanoo, managed to film a ghost on one of her adventures around Pakistan. It was like a beam of light, gliding down the stairs of a rickety, old house in Chitral that Nanoo (who filmed anything that moved, dead or alive) had stayed in. From then on, the boys were hooked.

Neither had ever seen a ghost themselves although Saif tried to convince his brother that one night, out by the stables of Nurpur, their farm, he'd seen the ghost of a headless horseman wandering by. Wisely, Taimur didn't believe him but poor Ditta, who helped take care of them, did, and ran screaming into the house.

Still, the twins' room was crowded with ghost lore and hunting equipment— an electroplasmic reader that Leeloo Khaloo had sent them from London (to measure static levels of electricity in case the ghosts were invisible), a camera that could be switched onto infrared to see things that moved in the dark, and some small laser alarms that would make a noise when something passed through the air.

Saif and Taimur had begged and pleaded for all these things for over a year, forgoing their allowance to buy their equipment. The twins were serious about ghost hunting and they swore that when they finally got to see one they would be ready, get it all on camera, and would become famous for proving the existence of ghosts!

What neither of them realized was that their wishes would soon be granted. ▪

OXFORD
UNIVERSITY PRESS

The Mystery of the Aagnee Ruby

Dear Jacob + Conrad,

MAHA KHAN PHILLIPS

I think you are too grown up)
now for this book but
here's a copy none the less!

Love,

Maha

(Ro's mum)

OXFORD
UNIVERSITY PRESS

OXFORD
UNIVERSITY PRESS

Great Clarendon Street, Oxford OX2 6DP

Oxford University Press is a department of the University of Oxford.
It furthers the University's objective of excellence in research, scholarship,
and education by publishing worldwide in

Oxford   New York
Auckland   Cape Town   Dar es Salaam   Hong Kong   Karachi   Kuala Lumpur
Madrid   Melbourne   Mexico City   Nairobi   New Delhi   Shanghai   Taipei   Toronto

With offices in
Argentina   Austria   Brazil   Chile   Czech Republic   France   Greece
Guatemala   Hungary   Italy   Japan   Poland   Portugal   Singapore
South Korea   Switzerland   Turkey   Ukraine   Vietnam

ISBN: 978-0-19-547768-9

Sixth Impression 2014

Printed in Pakistan at
The Times Press (Pvt.) Ltd, Karachi
Published by
Ameena Saiyid, Oxford University Press
No. 38, Sector 15, Korangi Industrial Area,
PO Box 8214, Karachi-74900, Pakistan

Chapter Two

A Strange Little Girl
called Amina

Two hours later, Saif and Taimur emerged from their bedroom, their hair still wet from their showers. They were both wearing crisp, white shalwar kameez.

With sighs of resignation, (as loud as possible so Baba might hear them as they walked past study and rescue them) they entered the drawing room. They could already hear Aunty Jum Jum's deep, manly voice. She was talking about how much she loved Amla hair oil.

'Ahh, there you are children,' said their mother with a slight edge in her voice that said they had taken their time getting there.'

Saif shot his brother a look. Now they would have to stay at least an extra fifteen minutes to make up for their tardiness! He looked longingly at the tea tray, filled with samosas, leftover chocolate cake from Baba's birthday party, and his favourite—chocolate éclairs. But first, he would have to go and greet Aunty Jum Jum, who was sitting on the armchair on the other side of the room with her arms outstretched, and a gleeful look on her face.

This time, when they walked over, Saif pushed Taimur forward first, laughing to himself when Taimur shrieked. When it was his turn, Saif stuck out his hand and mumbled hello, hoping that would be enough. But Aunty Jum Jum wasted no time in bundling him into her arms. If anything, she had grown wider since the last time the boys had seen her! A second hairy mole now graced her chin—this was something new, Saif observed as he felt himself being practically lifted off the floor and into her embrace.

'Oh boys,' she gushed, 'don't you look so *cute* in your *beautiful* kameezes? I was *just* telling your Mama how I couldn't *wait* to see you again and take you into my arms!'

A few kisses and slurps later, the boys were free. They ran behind their mother, who gave them an amused, understanding look. They both mumbled polite answers to all of Aunty Jum Jum's questions, trying to keep their distance.

'Tell me now boys,' she said as she waddled over to the tea tray to pile up on samosas, 'do you like cricket?'

Mama looked slightly concerned—Aunty Jum Jum had put twelve samosas on her plate—she quickly rang the bell for Ditta and asked him to bring some more so they wouldn't run out.

'Yes,' they both mumbled, looking down on the floor.

'Do you like riding?'

'Yes,' they mumbled again, determined not to go into details. But Aunty Jum Jum was not to be dissuaded, and each reply was met with a battery of questions until, with a contented sigh, she leaned back into her chair, which groaned under her weight.

Saif and Taimur decided that this was their cue. They were free! They made a rush for the tea tray to grab the cheese sandwiches that Ditta had just brought in. Maybe Mama would let them take their plates to their bedroom.

'You know, Tia, your boys look *nothing* like each other,' Aunty Jum Jum said. Mama twirled a spoon through her tea and tried to keep a straight face.

Saif and Taimur sighed. Every time it was the same. Aunty Jum Jum refused to understand the concept of non-identical twins, twins who were born at the same time but who did not look the same. Each time she visited they

OXFORD
UNIVERSITY PRESS

would be paraded in front of her so that she could gasp over their similarities and differences.

Taimur took after their mother and was tall and thin, with dark brown hair that flopped over his eyes most of the time. He had a smile that his mother called angelic, a word that upset him so much that he spent most of his time trying to remember to scowl like Vin Diesel in XXX.

Saif was broad and had light, curly hair. He was the spitting image of his father, and when he smiled all the adults grimaced, because his smile was full of mischief. He was constantly in trouble, and had a great knack for convincing Taimur to participate in his wild antics. Only last month he had dragged Taimur out of bed at three in the morning: the two of them had gone up to the cook's room, set firecrackers off under his bed and raced out. The poor old cook, had been convinced that the house was being attacked and screamed his head off! Mama had not been happy. She had massaged the sides of her head for weeks after, because her headache would not go away.

Together, the twins wreaked havoc. Lahore would never recover from Saif and Taimur, Baba liked to say, but secretly, they knew that every time Mama scolded them harshly for something they had done, their Baba would laugh about it later.

But where was Baba when you really needed him? How long would they have to sit there and be polite?

Not very long at all, as it turned out. Both boys were surprised when they heard footsteps behind them.

'Come on *boys*, you must meet my *darling* little niece.' Aunty Jum Jum grabbed both their arms and marched them to the front door, where a girl about their age was standing.

'This is my little Amina, boys. Isn't she a dear?' Aunty Jum Jum gushed.

The boys stared at the mousy little girl in front of them. If possible, she looked even unhappier than they did. She barely said hello, her brown eyes

OXFORD
UNIVERSITY PRESS

7

kept darting left and right, looking for escape. She was dressed entirely in black; black combat boots, black jeans, and a black T-shirt with a picture of a dagger on it.

'Didn't I tell you what a *lovely* garden the Noons had? Have you seen their peacock and the deer at the back? It's all the boys you know, they simply *love* animals.' Really, Aunty Jum Jum was too much.

But unlike Saif and Taimur, Amina did not seem to be intimidated by Aunty Jum Jum's bulk. 'The peacock wasn't doing anything and the deer was asleep, and I thought you said we were going somewhere exciting, Jum Jum Aunty.'

Everyone was quiet for a moment. The twins looked at Amina with new respect. Imagine someone talking back to Aunty Jum Jum, the old battleaxe!

Eventually, Mama began to fiddle with her teacup, a sure sign that she was irritated. She asked the twins to go and play with Amina in their room, while she and Aunty Jum Jum talked. Grateful for the escape, they raced to their room. The boys were a little disheartened about having to spend time with the odd girl, but they were thrilled to be away from the drawing room!

Their happiness didn't last long though. They tried their best to be friendly to Amina, but the girl was simply being rude. They asked her if she wanted to watch TV, and she said 'No'. They showed her where their Archie comic collection was, and she sniffed in disdain.

Taimur pulled his brother aside. 'Maybe she's one of those, you know, *girly* girls who just like playing with Barbie dolls and frilly things—you know, like Aisha Aunty's daughter.'

Saif frowned. 'Well, she doesn't really look like a girly girl does she? I mean, she's wearing trousers and a T-shirt and those big, sturdy boots even though it's the middle of the summer, and she's all in black!'

It was true that Amina did not look like she would enjoy playing with Barbie dolls. With a discontented sigh, she flopped onto the cane chair in the corner of the bedroom, her legs hanging across one of its arms, looking contemptuously at all she surveyed.

 OXFORD
UNIVERSITY PRESS

'Well, if she's going to be like that, I say we ignore her,' said Saif huffily.

Taimur nodded in agreement, and the two of them sat opposite her on Saif's bed, with their backs turned. They eagerly continued reading their new book, 'Searching for the Paranormal: ghostly presences on the Indian subcontinent'.

'Just look at that one!' Taimur pointed at a drawing of a decapitated man in white, walking down a rickety, old staircase, holding his head in his hands. 'Imagine seeing him in the middle of the night, he would give you a scare, I bet!'

Saif looked closely. 'It says here that the most paranormal activity ever recorded in this part of the world is in a house up north—in Naran! Maybe

one day Mama and Baba will take us to see it, what do you think? Apparently it's a big ol' house that was built almost a hundred and fifty years ago at the time of the Raj, by a British governor whose ghost still haunts the place!'

'Mama and Baba will absolutely refuse to take us somewhere like that,' sighed Taimur. 'And it does say nobody has ever seen the ghost, just heard him. It could turn out to be like when Kamila Khala told us there was a ghost of a dead lizard that crawled up and down her bedroom wall—we sat waiting for it forever, didn't we? And we never saw it, and poor Jo Jo went into palpitations—you know how scared of *chipkalees* she is!'

'You fool!' replied Saif. 'She was joking. And *you* were the only one who fell for it! If you remember, I got bored after a few minutes and walked away! You were there for hours.'

Taimur chose to ignore his brother and concentrate on the book. He was now reading a story about a ghost wolf that lived in Balochistan and killed little children.

'I've seen the ghost, actually.'

Both brothers turned around. Amina, for once, was sitting up and had something to say. She stared at them both intensely, waiting for one of them to respond. The boys found her stare very disconcerting and, despite himself, Taimur felt a shudder go through him.

After her earlier behaviour, Saif and Taimur had intended to ignore her. But the idea of hearing about ghosts was very appealing. Too appealing finally for Taimur, who turned and sat on the other side of the bed, and said in his most disinterested voice, yawning for special effect, 'Just *what* are you talking about?'

'The Governor's House in Naran. It's actually called Kohistan House. I know what goes on there.' Amina's voice sounded strange, hollow. She spoke slowly, as if thinking about every word. 'He's a ghost that's very old and kills people off, one by one. But first, he plays with them. He makes their things disappear, makes them see things, and then poof!—they die, just like that.'

 OXFORD
UNIVERSITY PRESS

Taimur felt another shiver run down his spine. Amina was just being ridiculous, trying to make them feel uncomfortable. 'Oh yeah, and who died and made you the expert on Kohistan House, huh?' he lashed back. Saif couldn't help but snort in amusement.

Amina said nothing. The strange little girl's eyes narrowed. She got up and went to the door. Then, just before she left, she looked back. 'My parents. My parents died. I know what goes on in that house you see, because I live there.' With that, she stalked out of the room, leaving Saif and Taimur to stare at each other in shocked silence. ▪

Chapter Three

The Aagnee Ruby

It took the boys a moment to react. 'Well, don't just sit there. We'd better go down after her!' Saif said, scrambling to his feet.

By the time they got downstairs, they could hear voices by the front door. It was Mama saying goodbye to Aunty Jum Jum. Had Amina said something to her aunt? Is that why they were leaving?

But no, it was clear from the beaming smile Aunty Jum Jum was giving them, arms outstretched (again), that Amina had not said anything to anyone.

OXFORD
UNIVERSITY PRESS

Instead she just stood quietly beside the door, with her gaze somewhere near the floor. The twins didn't know quite what to make of her. What shocked them most, however, was when Mama leaned over and gave Amina's hand a little squeeze. 'Goodbye, dear. You take care of yourself, OK?'

The boys were stunned. Earlier, it was obvious that Mama disapproved of Amina. And now here she was, telling the girl to come back anytime. 'Not if I have anything to do with it,' muttered Saif under his breath.

Taimur poked him in the side. 'Pay attention,' he whispered. 'Don't you see that this is our chance? If we can get to know Amina, maybe Mama will let us visit the house and we can see the ghost for ourselves.'

'But you heard what she said—she's barking mad!' whispered Saif furiously.

'Now boys, come and give your Aunty a big kiss! I am going to miss you both so much!'

Oh God! Aunty Jum Jum. *Again.* The twins, feeling a little bit guilty about the way they treated Amina, subjected themselves to further kisses and cheek pulling. When Aunty Jum Jum finally stepped into her car, they sighed with relief.

Before Amina could follow, Saif pulled her arm. 'Listen, we're … we're sorry. We didn't know.'

Amina gave them both a sad smile. 'Nobody ever does,' she said, getting into the car. As the car pulled out of the driveway, they watched her little face twist back towards them, staring from the back seat with small, inscrutable, dark eyes.

Later that night, when Mama and Baba were asleep, the twins sat up in bed, whispering. 'Somehow, we've got to convince Mama and Baba to let us spend part of the summer in Naran,' said Taimur. 'I feel sorry for Amina. She said both her parents were dead. She's obviously a bit mad and thinks the ghost kills people. Maybe, if we catch this ghost, we can help her.'

Saif nodded his head. 'Bhai, it's strange but, I ... believed her. I think ... I think something's going on. She needs our help. The only question is, how are we going to get to Naran?'

'Don't look at me; you're the one with all the bright ideas!'

'We'll figure something out,' said Saif. 'In the meantime, we'd better read this book and get prepared!' He grabbed a torch from under his bed (hidden there so Mama wouldn't find it and realize that the twins spent most of their nights reading under the covers). The boys got under the sheets and started to read. To their delight, they found that a whole chapter of their book was devoted to the house in Naran.

The Kohistan House Mystery

Kohistan House stands alone, on top of a steep hill close to Naran. Though there is one other house on Kimchoo Hill, built around the same period (1862), the area is quite isolated. It is fifteen miles to the nearest train station or shop. The house is said to have recorded the most paranormal activity of any in the Indian subcontinent, but to date, nobody has actually sighted the ghostly spectre of Governor John Marcham, the British envoy who is believed to walk its corridors. Instead, residents are plagued with strange noises, moving objects, and bizarre and often fatal accidents.

During the British Raj, Governor Marcham built the house as a summer home for his wife, Gertrude, and named it after the mountains of Naran which he grew to love. He governed the Naran region in the decade between 1861 and 1871, and built-up a close friendship with Maharajah Duleep Bargoza, (Bunny to his friends), ruler of Naran.

Sadly, anger towards the British and their cronies led to the rebellion of Jam Git in 1872, and 'Bunny' was killed. Only hours later, Marcham also died, murdered in very mysterious circumstances in his own home. His wife and young son, however, were able to escape, and made their way back to England, along with their maid, Betty.

The Aagnee Ruby—A Link to the Curse of Kohistan House?

Nobody knows why Marcham haunts his old summer home, but one clue might be in the strange disappearance of the Aagnee Ruby.

Historians will remember that the precious ruby, the like and size of which has never been equalled, is said to possess magic powers, to have literally been forged from the fire of men's hearts. The Maharajah's family claimed that the ruby was its lifeblood, keeping the family strong and healthy. Each generation was told to protect it or die trying to do so. One unfortunate would-be thief, a cousin to the royal family, had his eyes gouged out just for looking at it too much.

Historians believe that the Maharajah suspected his life was in danger before the rebellion. Bunny may have given the jewel to his trusted friend, Governor Marcham, for safekeeping. When Bunny died—(he was killed by an angry mob), his family accused Marcham of having stolen the ruby. The Maharajah's wife swore that Marcham would be cursed for the rest of his days because of the ruby's mystic powers: it belonged to the Bargoza family and would bring tragedy to anyone who tried to take it.

Only hours later, Governor Marcham was found dead. All the rooms in Kohistan House were locked. Nobody could have got in or out, and so the mystery of his murder has never been solved. Did Marcham hide the Aagnee Ruby to keep it for himself? Did someone take revenge? Does his ghost really haunt Kohistan House as punishment for the theft? This author attempted to find out the truth for himself, but was told in no uncertain terms by its current occupiers that any attempt to access the house would result in the loss of his limbs. Thus, the Mystery of Kohistan House remains exactly that.

'My goodness!' whispered Taimur when finally, at dawn, they finished reading. 'A ghost, a betrayal, a curse, and a treasure. What more can you ask for!'

'Let's just get there first,' muttered the now sleepy Saif, pushing his brother off his bed and back into his own. 'We'll have to figure out how, tomorrow.' ▪

OXFORD
UNIVERSITY PRESS

Chapter Four

As Luck Would Turn Out

In the end, it turned out to be easier than expected. While Saif and Taimur prepared to battle it out with Mama and to get permission to go to Naran, Mama was secretly hoping to persuade them to spend a week there as well!

Once Aunty Jum Jum had told her Amina's sad history, Mama was convinced that something had to be done—Amina had to have some people her own age to talk to, otherwise she would go truly mad!

The twins couldn't believe their luck when, at breakfast, Mama told them that they would be sacrificing a week to go up north with her to keep Amina company.

The boys tried to hide their glee. 'Alright Mama, if you insist,' said Taimur calmly, spreading jam on a piece of toast. Saif's face was deadpan.

Mama, who was not used to the boys *ever* caving in on anything, barrelled forward, convinced that there would be opposition. 'The poor child is an orphan. She lost her father less than a year ago, and her mother died only a few months before, both in extremely strange accidents! Jum Jum tells me that Amina spends most of her year in boarding school, and only goes to Naran for the summers. Even then, she's cooped up in that ghastly old house with her bookish uncle and only an older cousin for company! She's never had a chance to meet children her own age, poor thing, and you two are going to grow up and go to Naran and enjoy it!'

'Whatever you say Mama,' said Saif, trying to keep a straight face.

'Now I know you wanted those polo lessons ...'

'No,' Taimur said quickly. 'You're right. We should be able to take a week out to help someone else; we can do the lessons when we get back.'

Mama's mouth dropped open. Two minutes earlier, she had been ready for the biggest mutiny possible. She imagined both children would be screaming at the loss of a week of their precious summer holidays. Now, however, they were as meek as lambs! For a second, a horrible thought crossed her mind, and her eyes narrowed.

'And just what is it that you two are up to?'

Both boys gave her their most angelic smiles.

Mama sighed. 'Alright, don't tell me. But sooner or later, you know I'll find out.'

She spent a few minutes telling them all about the north of Pakistan, and how beautiful it was, with its mountains and rivers and valleys. She explained that Amina lived miles from the village, and was quite secluded in her house. 'But they've got a river at the bottom of the garden, and apparently you can go trekking, and drive up to see the glaciers …'

Both boys nodded politely, and Mama arched an eyebrow. She was sure that the glaciers at least would have excited them—but no, they evidently had other things on their minds. 'Very well,' she sighed. 'You can be excused.'

The boys jumped up from the table and ran to their room.

Later, when Baba asked Mama how the boys had taken the news of their trip, she shrugged. 'They seem really happy, actually.' Baba snorted with laughter. 'Then it's official. They're definitely up to something! You'd better be careful!'

Mama frowned. 'I only wish you would hurry up and finish your work so I didn't have to go alone with them!' She put her head in her hands. 'Oh God! It's going to be utter chaos.'

Her prediction turned out to be true. Saif and Taimur started arguing the minute breakfast was over about what they would be taking with them. 'Our

'Ghost Hunting for Dummies' book says to bring a camera to record ectoplasm movements—that's the misty stuff that ghosts leave behind when they walk around. We also need torches—lots of torches! And what about this—an EMF detector—that's a device to measure the electromagnetic fields in the area. And look, here's an EMF stun gun, to stun a ghost so he freezes!' Saif said in excitement.

His brother shook his head. 'You're crazy. Where are we going to get something like that? We're just going to have to skip on some of the EMF thingy whatsits, and find our own way to capture ghosts.'

Eventually they compromised and settled on taking a compass along because their laser lights were too big to carry. Apparently, its needle would start to shake and move if a ghostly presence was passing by. Saif sulked for a day, wanting to 'borrow' Baba's video camera for the occasion. With a sigh, Taimur made him put it back in Baba's study before they were caught.

Meanwhile, Mama was also making big preparations. Winter clothes were brought down from the storeroom and washed because even though it was summer, the mountains were so high that it would be cold. Sturdy hiking boots were bought for both boys and for Mama. Because of his work, Baba could not come along on the trip, but he managed to find some of his old fishing rods and spent several evenings in the garden showing the boys how to cast a fishing line.

'Just so you're not complete amateurs when you get there,' he laughed.

So caught up were they in the preparations that neither brother realized that almost two weeks had gone by, and the time to leave was upon them. Barely able to contain their excitement on the actual day, they said goodbye to Baba, piled into the jeep with Mama, and set out on the long journey. They drove all the way to Abbotabad where they spent the night with a friend, and then onto Mansehra, Shogran, and past Siri Paya. The roads became uneven, rough, and bumpy as the scenery began to change and they started to drive up from the foothills of the mountains.

Saif, not the best travellers, very soon began to feel carsick during the second part of the journey, and the car had to stop regularly, so he could leap out and dive for bushes on the side of the road. It was not a pretty sight, especially because Taimur spent most of the journey laughing at his poor brother.

They played Snap and 'I spy with my little eye' as the hours crawled on and the roads began to narrow even more. Their constant enquiries of 'Are we nearly there yet?' prompted Mama to squeeze her eyes shut and shake her head.

When they began to fight over who would get to use their PSP2 first, Mama had had enough.

'Both of you be quiet. Forget about the stupid machine. Just look out the window and see what you're missing!'

With nothing else to do, the boys began to pay attention to the scenery outside and were stunned. Below them in the valley was the most beautiful lake they had ever seen; blue, completely clear and shimmering in the light. Reflected in the water were formidable but beautiful mountains with snow-capped peaks. 'The mountain in the distance is the Nanga Parbat peak,' explained Mama.

Saif was too amazed to even speak. 'It's incredible,' he whispered, pushing his nose against the window in his enthusiasm to see everything. Unfortunately, this prompted Taimur to complain that Saif was blocking his view, and the moment of peace was shattered again. Saif punched his brother on the nose Mam and a looked as though she was about to cry.

They passed Balakot and kept on driving. It had been over twelve hours since they started that morning, and Mama assured them that they would soon be in Naran. The road evened out a little, and Taimur gave a gasp as, in the distance—he saw a glacier. 'Look! Look!' he said excitedly and poked his brother in the ribs.

The jeep slowed right down. 'The glaciers can cause landslides,' explained Anwar the driver, carefully manoeuvring along the mountain roads.

OXFORD
UNIVERSITY PRESS

'Who are you? What do you want?'

Saif and Taimur immediately stepped in front of their mother, prepared for the worst.

But then the man was shunted sideways by a rather heavy bulk. 'Nasir Ali, *what* have I told you about answering the door—*really*, you frighten *all* our visitors away with that scowl of yours!'

The twins never thought they would have a reason to be *happy* to see Aunty Jum Jum, but there she was, in a blue dressing gown, with large black curlers in her hair, beaming at them. They were so relieved they could have kissed her! Obviously, Mama felt the same way because she launched herself immediately on her friend.

Aunty Jum Jum laughed in delight. 'Well, come on in then, you'll catch your death of cold outside! Ignore Nasir Ali. He's worked as the *chowkidar* here for so long, and we've all grown used to his strangeness. The *bijlee* has gone out again with the storm so we'll have to make do with the kerosene lamps.'

Aunty Jum Jum did not stop talking in her excitement and, meekly, they followed her into the house, both boys trying to stay well clear of Nasir Ali in the hallway—the man looked like he ate children for breakfast!

'Sorry we arrived so late,' said Mama. 'The roads were very bad.'

'Don't be silly, don't be silly,' replied Aunty Jum Jum jovially. 'We're so excited to have you here. Now stay close. It's easy to get confused in the darkness.'

She was right. It was hard to see much. Saif, who had spent most of the day throwing up, was exhausted, and walked around like a zombie. Taimur was much more alert though. He soon realized how easy it would be to get lost in Kohistan House. Aunty Jum Jum escorted them through so many narrow corridors and hallways, turning left at one, right at another, and left again at the next. It was as if the inside of the house was a maze and, with no lights, it was impossible to see where they were. Eventually, they found themselves in a cosy little living room, where a fire blazed cheerfully. Nasir Ali followed them in with several kerosene lamps, which added some light.

'There we are now,' Aunty Jum Jum sighed, placing her heavy bulk on a chair by the fire, and motioning for them to do the same. On the table a banquet was already laid out, and both boys felt their stomachs growl.

'It was so late, I thought some food, something light, to fill you up before bed …' said Aunty Jum Jum.

This was light food? The table was practically heaving with chicken, *keema parathas*, *daal* and chutney, and fresh hot *roti*. On the side was a thermos full of sweet, hot tea. After eating, everyone felt relaxed and realized how tired they were.

Aunty Jum Jum seemed to understand, showing them to two separate bedrooms, one on either side of the small living room. One was for Mama, the other for the boys. 'Don't let the fires go out—you'll freeze!' she warned, and bid them all goodnight. The boys began fighting over who would get the bed closer to the fire in their room, but the argument ended quickly when Mama told them she would kill them both if they didn't go to sleep.

In the end, they turned down their lamp and went to their room quietly. Saif fell asleep immediately, but it took Taimur a few minutes longer. He suddenly thought how strange it was that, even though they arrived late, neither Amina, nor her uncle who lived with her were there to greet them. With the flame in the lamp turned low, the room was cast in strange shadows, and he felt … nervous somehow.

He was just starting to doze off when he heard a strange creaking sound coming from the fireplace. Taimur blinked. It wasn't possible. It was … 'Saif, Bhai, wake up, wake up!' he whispered furiously. He leapt out of bed as fast as he could and shook his brother.

Saif groaned. '*Kya*? I'm so tired, leave me alone!' He tried to pull his quilt over his head.

'The … it's the ghost. It's the ghost!'

Saif's eyes snapped open immediately. 'Where? You better not be joking!'

Taimur said nothing, just pointed a trembling finger towards the fireplace.

There, coming out of the fire, was a green, fluorescent hand just dangling amidst all the black brick and pieces of kindling and wood. It fell to the ground and crawled out of the fireplace towards them.

Both boys fell back, shrieking.

The hand flexed its fingers in a sinister fashion, shaking its index finger from side to side. Then it turned around and crawled back to the fireplace. A few seconds later, it was gone.

'Allah help us,' Taimur whispered.

'Quickly, turn up the light in the kerosene lamp,' Saif said. Taimur grabbed the lamp and together, nervously, they walked towards the fireplace. On the floor by the fireplace was a strange, green substance.

'Ectoplasm,' Saif said in a shaking voice.

Taimur bent down for a further look, and then stood up, a strange expression on his face. 'I think we're being conned, Bhai.'

'What are you talking about?'

'Look closer.'

The brothers crouched down, looking carefully at the green substance.

'Do you see?' asked Taimur.

'See what?'

'Remember last year, when we did our science projects?'

'Remember? How can I forget? You're the science geek in the family, with all your electronics and things. Tell me what's going on!'

'I built a calculator.'

'Yes.'

'A glow in the dark calculator.'

'Yes, I remember, you used that fluorescent spray paint and won first prize. How long are we supposed to congratulate you for it? I for one think it's about time you stopped showing off!'

'Silly!' said Taimur, dipping his finger into the green sludge. 'Look!' He showed his finger to his brother.

'Why, it's only glow in the dark spray!'

'Exactly!'

'But the hand …'

'Simple robotics. Remember the hand Nina Nana bought us once, the remote-controlled one that could do creepy movements and things?'

'You're saying it was one of those?' Saif asked.

Taimur shrugged. 'I don't know. All I'm saying is that the stuff on this floor is definitely not ectoplasm. It's spray paint that's slightly melted from the fire. Trust me, I spent enough time using the stuff last year.'

Saif sighed, sitting on the bed. 'It looks like we're going to have to be extra careful, Bhai.'

'Why, because someone thinks we'll fall for a stupid joke like this?'

'No,' said Saif quietly. 'It's because somebody doesn't want us to be here. Someone's trying to scare us away.' ▪

Chapter Six

Uncle Hamid and his Moths

T he next morning, Taimur almost wished someone had succeeded in chasing them away. Amina's Uncle Hamid was the rudest man either brother had ever met!

Mama woke both boys up early in the morning, and made sure they made it to the dining room for breakfast on time. Saif and Taimur were tired. They had sat up most of the night talking, and decided that the best thing to do was to pretend that nothing had happened. Whoever wanted to chase them away wouldn't do it that easily! The boys didn't know Amina very well, but they knew that she was lonely up here, and sad. They didn't think she would be cruel enough to play such a practical joke which meant that either her cousin, or her uncle, were up to no good.

Amina, her older cousin Hassan, and Aunty Jum Jum were already sitting around the breakfast table when they arrived. The twins were on their best behaviour, all the while keeping their eyes open to try and figure out who could be the culprit from the night before. They mumbled their hellos to Amina, who was still wearing all black. They shook Hassan's hand.

Hassan smiled broadly and his eyes twinkled. The twins liked him immediately. Like Amina, he spent most of the year in boarding school, but was seventeen and soon going to America for further studies. He was a large, red-cheeked, good-humoured boy with just their taste for adventure—he told them that he knew every inch of the mountainside around them, and spent most of his summer exploring old caves or climbing the cliffs. Hassan had even been bitten by a shark once when scuba-diving in the Florida Keys,

OXFORD
UNIVERSITY PRESS

where his mother lived! The twins were impressed, and more impressed when Hassan started teasing Amina about her 'Goth' look—Amina's face lit into a huge smile and she started laughing—it was obvious that she idolized her older cousin.

Then Uncle Hamid, Hassan's father, walked into the room. The laughter, and the conversation, stopped.

A tall, bald man with a goatee and glasses, Uncle Hamid had a sharp, patrician nose, which made it hard to tell whether he seemed to look down on people naturally or because he really meant it. He scowled at them all before sitting down to breakfast. 'You must be those Noons Jum Jum talks so much about.

Eager to see Naran, eh? Isn't Lahore good enough entertainment these days?' He was obviously trying to be funny.

The boys looked at Mama, unsure how to answer. Mama just smiled politely and thanked Uncle Hamid for inviting them to stay. 'I didn't invite you,' he snapped. 'Jum Jum insisted that you come. It's a most inconvenient time for me, actually, my moths are about to hatch.'

Moths? What on earth was the man talking about?

'Ignore my father,' Hassan said, all his earlier friendliness vanishing, his body tense. 'He breeds and studies moths; it's his hobby. He prefers their company to the company of his own family. Isn't that right, Pa?'

Uncle Hamid did not even bother to look at his son. Instead, he opened up a newspaper and began to read.

The twins were shocked. How could the man be so rude to his guests? What on earth was going on? Taimur glanced quickly at Amina to make sure she was all right but she just sat there, calmly eating her scrambled eggs on toast. Whatever the relationship was between father and son, she was obviously used to Uncle Hamid's rudeness.

Unfortunately for them, Mama wasn't. 'Well, we don't want to intrude. We'll stay the afternoon but make our way back to Lahore in a few hours,' she said politely, but firmly.

Aunty Jum Jum started to wail in protest. 'Oh, but you only just got here! You mustn't leave! We're all so excited to have you!' Slightly hysterically, she gave Uncle Hamid a prod with her elbow. 'Aren't we happy to have them Hamid?'

Uncle Hamid just shrugged. 'Do whatever you want,' he practically snarled, and left the table.

There was nothing in the world that would make her stay, Mama thought angrily, until, from the corner of her eye, she spotted Amina. Amina was looking down at her plate. A single tear escaped and ran down her cheeks. Mama's heart went out to the girl.

 OXFORD
UNIVERSITY PRESS

'We'll see,' she said, not wanting to break Amina's heart any more.

Saif and Taimur let out sighs of relief. They shot each other a look. They had better crack on with finding the ghost, because time was limited!

'Please forgive my father,' sighed Hassan, getting up from the table. 'He's been … difficult ever since Aunty Ayla, Amina's mother, passed away. It's been hard on him. She was his only sister.'

'We understand,' said Mama quietly. She was looking at Amina, who had put down her fork, and leaving her scrambled eggs uneaten.

'Good, everything is fine now,' said Aunty Jum Jum, clapping her hands. 'Hassan, Amina, why don't you show the boys around? I bet they'd love to see the river. In fact, I'll pack you a picnic lunch, and you can go do some trout fishing, what do you say?'

Saif and Taimur let out whoops of joy. After all of Baba's lessons with the rods, they were dying to go fishing! Hassan laughed. 'Come on,' he said, patting Taimur on the back. 'Let's get you guys kitted out.'

'Actually, I'm a vegetarian,' Amina said quietly. 'I think fishing is cruel.'

'Oh, come on cousin, don't be like that,' said Hassan, ruffling her hair. Amina looked like she was about to cry.

'Tell you what,' said Taimur, feeling sorry for her. 'Amina, what would you like to do?'

'I really like painting.'

'Then how about you and I do some sketching and painting while Hassan and Saif catch some fish?'

'Bhai,' said Saif, taking him aside. 'I feel bad. You shouldn't have to baby sit …'

'We're here to *help* her, remember? Plus, this way, we can ask them both questions and find out what's going on.'

'You're right,' said Saif. 'The sooner we figure it out the better!' ▪

Chapter Seven

The Devil's Mouth

It was a beautiful day, and the boys were thrilled to be outside. They wore their hardiest jeans and thick woollen sweaters because it was cold. They waited in the front driveway, Saif with a fishing rod in his hand and Taimur with a sketchbook. Hassan had gone to get supplies and Amina, some paints and pencils.

'You know, Kohistan House is really not that creepy when the sun is shining on it—look,' said Saif.

Taimur looked at the house. In the daytime, it was beautiful. Half of the front was covered in thick green and pink ivy, and on every side was a field of yellow daffodils. On the second floor was a large balcony, covered in plants and flowerpots. Dozens of multicoloured butterflies fluttered about, attracted to the flowers. 'Wow,' he whispered.

'Yeah. It's pretty amazing that this beautiful place could be haunted.'

Taimur frowned, pushing his hair out of his eyes, where it had fallen as usual. 'Well, maybe it isn't haunted.'

'What do you mean?'

'Last night was a hoax, right?'

'Yeah, so?' asked Saif.

'So maybe the same person who wants to get rid of us wants to make sure nobody else comes snooping around. Who's going to want to hang out in a haunted place, after all?'

'Well, that would be disappointing. We came here to find a ghost.'

'Hmm … maybe we'll find something else instead.'

'What do you mean?'

'Nothing,' said Taimur, shaking his head. 'It's far too early to jump to conclusions.'

'I wonder who owns the place,' said Saif, looking up at the house, using the palm of his hand as a screen against the sun. 'I mean, did it belong to Amina's parents, or does it belong to Uncle Hamid?'

'Half and half, actually,' said Hassan, creeping up behind them. The boys jumped, and Saif reddened.

'Oh, no, don't be embarrassed. People often wonder. An old house like this is worth a lot of money. It makes people think the family's loaded. Actually, we're not.'

'We just thought …' said Taimur.

Hassan laughed, and put his arms around the two boys. 'It belonged to our grandparents—Amina's and mine. Amina's mother inherited half, and my father the other half. Of course, now half of it is Amina's.'

Saif looked admiringly at Hassan's khaki fishing bag which had little pockets on the sides for tackle and bait. 'Does your father live here all year round?'

'Now he does, yes. We used to live in Florida though, before my parents split up.'

'Oh,' said Saif, colouring again. 'Sorry to hear it.'

'Well, I'm not. Those two were useless together. This way, I get the best of both worlds. Naran and Miami. Now are we going to sit here all day or are we going fishing? Look, there's Amina. Let's go!'

Amina came shyly out of the house, carrying a straw basket containing a canvas and some paints. She was still in her black combat boots, black jeans,

and T-shirt. This time, the T-shirt had a skull on it. 'Nasir Ali's going to bring the picnic lunch. We just need to tell him where we'll be,' she said.

'The Devil's Mouth, of course, where else?' said Hassan.

'The Devil's Mouth?' asked Saif.

OXFORD
UNIVERSITY PRESS

Hassan laughed, and put his hand on Saif's shoulder. 'Come on, we'll show you.'

They walked down the hill, and the boys realized just how inaccessible Kohistan House really was. It would be quite a steep walk back up, and they'd walked for at least twenty minutes before the hill flattened out. Then they came to a complete stop.

'This isn't a hill, it's a cliff,' whispered Saif, looking down a hundred feet below, where a river gushed past furiously against sharp rocks.

'Yes. Kimchoo Hill is surrounded by cliffs on three sides. There's only one road down, and that's the way you fellows drove yesterday,' said Hassan.

'So how do we get down?' asked Taimur.

'With a little Northern ingenuity,' said Hassan, smiling mischievously. 'Come on, follow me.' He tossed his fishing bag over his shoulder and, whistling, led them to a wooden box a few feet away. 'It's a cable lift.'

'A cable lift?' Taimur blinked twice. The wooden box would barely hold the four of them, and it was already creaking under the weight of its old ropes and pulleys. It didn't look safe at all.

'Yeah,' said Hassan, grinning, looking very pleased with himself. 'It's somewhere between a cable car and a lift. It's been around for over fifty years. You guys aren't scared or anything?'

'Of course not,' said Saif immediately. More than anything, Saif hated to be called a coward. Whatever the danger, he would always barrel forward, without thinking. Taimur was the one who stopped and measured up the risks. He often had to calm his feisty brother down.

Hassan pressed a hand against his stomach and burst out laughing. 'I'm sorry,' he giggled. 'I just couldn't resist it! You should have seen your faces! Imagine going down in that old thing.'

'So it was a joke?' asked Taimur, exhaling with relief.

'Of course,' said Hassan. 'We're not that stupid. If we walk a bit further, the cliff turns left, and there are some man-made stairs that go all the way down to the river.'

Hassan was right. They walked for a few more minutes and came to some thick, broad stairs. The stairs were carved out of the stone cliff. They were easy to climb down.

'Be careful though,' warned Hassan. 'Sometimes they can be slippery.'

Slowly they made their way down the cliff to the river bed. By the time they reached the bottom, Saif was beaming. 'Bhai, have you ever seen such beauty in your entire life?'

The river rumbled past them, icy cold from the nearby glacier, and frothing, like soda, every time it came across a boulder or obstacle. At various points on the cliffs, shrubs and trees had made their homes, so everything looked green. Taimur put his arm around his brother. 'It's something else, isn't it?'

Hassan, who was dressed in a khaki fishing vest, handed Saif a blue and green feathered fly. 'Here, the trout love this stuff.'

Amina shyly tugged on Taimur's jeans. 'Shall we go sit on that rock over there? It's a perfect place to paint.'

'Er, yeah, sure,' said Taimur, looking longingly at the river. Saif and Hassan had already rolled up their jeans, and, wearing high boots, waded their way in, casting back and forth with their rods, making swishing noises in the wind.

'You can fish, if you like,' said Amina.

Taimur turned to look at her. She looked crestfallen.

'No, I don't want to. I was just admiring the view.'

Amina beamed, and Taimur felt heartened. The poor girl seemed quite lost, out here. She needed all the support she could get!

 OXFORD
UNIVERSITY PRESS

They sat on the boulder, taking out paints and pencils. Taimur heard someone grunt behind him, and jumped when he saw Nasir Ali come limping by. Nasir Ali glared at him with his one good eye. He was carrying a heavy picnic hamper, and Taimur rushed to help him.

'Don't,' Nasir Ali snapped. 'Don't touch.'

Taimur gritted his teeth. What was wrong with everybody at Kohistan House? They were all so prickly! 'All right,' he said. 'Only trying to help.'

Nasir Ali stared at him for a moment, and then grunted again. He placed the basket on the ground beside them, and pulled out a thick, woollen blanket. On it, he put plates and cutlery, and a large thermos of tea. Then he used his hand to wipe away the sweat that had accumulated under his red turban. 'I will be on the other side; you just call when you're leaving.'

'Thank you, Nasir Ali,' said Amina. Taimur was shocked when the burly giant smiled back at her, flashing his gold tooth, before vanishing amongst the rocks.

'He's quite a fellow,' said Taimur.

Amina handed him a mug of steaming tea. 'Drink this… its cold out here. And don't mind Nasir Ali. He loved my parents. It was hard for him when they both died.'

Taimur looked at her awkwardly, unsure of what to say. They began to pick out pencils and paints. 'What shall we draw?'

Amina was quiet for a moment. 'I only paint one thing,' she said at last. 'The Devil's Mouth.'

'What's that?'

Amina pointed a finger eastwards. 'Look up there,' she said.

Taimur squinted, and looked. 'It looks like a cave. Wait, I have Baba's binoculars here. Let me see. Why, it's a cave, isn't it? But what an odd shape.'

'Yes,' said Amina, almost whispering. 'They look like fangs, don't they—those pieces of rock jutting out from the left and right.'

'That's why you call it the Devil's Mouth.'

'Yes.'

'I can see why you'd want to paint it. It's quite something, a fanged cave jutting out of the cliff wall like that. Have people ever explored it?'

'Yes,' said Amina quietly, looking down at her canvas.

'Does it go quite deep into the cliff?'

'Yes. There are smaller caves going for miles in every direction.'

'Hmm,' said Taimur. 'What an interesting place it would be to explore! How does one get there?'

'Oh,' said Amina in a strange voice. 'You have to climb. It's only safe for professional rock climbers. I've never been there, though I'd *really* like to see it.'

Taimur looked at her, surprised by the fervour in her voice. 'Maybe you'll see it, one day. Why don't you learn how to climb?'

'Uncle Hamid won't let me.'

'That seems a bit unfair, doesn't it? You can learn until you're good enough, can't you? I mean, I'm sure it takes a long while, but it's good to have goals … take me and my soccer. When I grow up, I want …'

'The last climber who went up there died,' said Amina, cutting him short. She had a strange look in her eyes, as it she was somewhere else.

'Really? How?'

'Nobody really knows, except the climbing rope was cut from above, and broke. Nobody else could have climbed up there, not without a rope, not without being seen. I think it was the ghost.'

'The ghost?'

'Marcham's ghost. He kills everyone.'

'Listen Amina, I'm sure …'

'It takes three point two seconds to fall to your death from the Devil's Mouth. Believe me, I've researched it. Can you imagine what a person must be thinking, in those final moments, before hitting the ground?'

'I can't,' said Taimur. 'But there's no point dwelling on it. The climber must have had a frayed rope and forgotten to check it, that's all.'

'No she didn't. She didn't have a frayed rope, because it was brand new. I should know. I was in the shop when she bought it. She was my mother, after all.' ▪

Chapter Eight

Fishing with Hassan

S aif shouted with excitement. 'I've got one, I've got one!'

Hassan came wading towards him. 'Let me see,' he said, grabbing Saif's rod. 'Wow, he's a beauty, and you reeled him in all by yourself! Congratulations!'

Saif beamed with happiness. This was turning out to be a fantastic day. Hassan had already caught three trout, and Saif had been feeling left out! Now that he'd managed to catch his own, he felt a sense of accomplishment. Hassan promised to show him how to clean and gut the fish. Then they were going to fry them, with some lemon and oil over a wood fire, and have them as part of their lunch. Hassan was so cool, knowing how to do these things! And Naran was so exciting!

'Come on,' said Hassan, wading back towards the dry river bank. 'I'm getting hungry. We'll clean and cook the fish here, so Amina doesn't see them and get upset. Then we'll join the others.'

Saif tried to hide his disappointment. He was dying to show his catch to Taimur!

Hassan smiled, as though reading his mind. 'There'll be other times. My Amina is … delicate. I don't want to hurt her.'

Saif nodded. 'She's been through a lot, hasn't she?'

'Yes,' replied Hassan, pulling a penknife out of his fishing bag. 'Gather some twigs for me, will you? We'll use them to start the fire.'

Saif began foraging around. 'You two seem to be very close,' he said.

Hassan looked up. 'We are. We're the only cousins in the family. And she's so much younger than me. I feel very protective towards her.'

Saif smiled. 'I know what you mean. We're very close to our cousin too, even though he's only four and a total pain. His name is Smooch.'

'That's a sort of an odd name, if you don't mind me saying so.'

Saif laughed. 'It's actually Rohan, but my Nanoo likes to give us all nicknames. We've got another cousin called Cubbie, too. We're sort of like a gang. We spend part of every summer together. In fact, we even call ourselves the CC Gang. CC stands for Clever Cousins.'

Hassan smiled. 'What fun that must be. I wish I had more relatives. It would have been great fun to set up my own gang when I was younger. But there was only Aunty Ayla and my father, and now of course, she's gone.'

Saif cleared his throat. 'What happened to Amina's parents, if you don't mind me asking?'

Hassan sat on his haunches and sighed. 'It's common knowledge. See that cave over there? No, that one—yes, with the fangs. It's called the Devil's Mouth. Aunty Ayla loved rock climbing—she was one of the best climbers in Pakistan—and one day she decided to climb up to the cave and explore it. Her rope wasn't secure and she fell and died.'

'But that's ... that's only a few feet from where we are now!' said Saif, shocked.

'Yes.'

'And you still come here, and you bring Amina!'

'What do you want us to do? Hide out in the house and pretend that life doesn't go on?' Hassan snapped.

Saif was quiet. 'I've offended you. I'm sorry.'

Hassan began to gut the fish. 'No, no you haven't, it's just such a sensitive topic, that's all. Amina's ... well, she's become a little strange since it happened. She seems to think the ghost did it. We're all trying to show her that life goes on, and that she has to deal with it. That her mother would have been happy to see her by the river. It was Aunty Ayla's favourite place in the world. She climbed the cliffs nearly everyday. The locals thought she was mad, but she loved it.'

Saif handed Hassan a pile of twigs. 'Do you believe there's a ghost?'

Hassan smiled grimly. 'Well, strange things *do* happen all the time. But a ghost wasn't responsible for Aunty Ayla's death. Nor was a ghost responsible for the fact that Uncle Haroon, Amina's father, had a heart attack while

OXFORD
UNIVERSITY PRESS

driving down the hill. He crashed his car, and died. These things just… happen I suppose. It's just bad luck.'

'Very bad luck,' said Saif, quietly.

Hassan smiled. 'Well you know what they say about luck, don't you?'

'What's that?'

'Sooner or later, it's got to change.'

Once the fish were ready, they started to walk to where Amina and Taimur had laid out the picnic lunch. Hassan began telling Saif how he'd swum with dolphins in Miami.

'Wow!' said Saif. 'You must really miss Florida. It sounds fantastic.'

Hassan's face darkened. 'It *was* fantastic. But then Papa went crazy and insisted on moving the family here. That's when my parents started having problems. Mom didn't want to come. She'd never liked it here.'

'Your dad moved here after Aunty Ayla died?'

'Oh no,' replied Hassan, shaking his head. 'A few months before. It's funny, you know. He got a letter from Aunty Alya one day, and the next thing we all know, he's quit his job in robotics and …'

'Robotics?' asked Saif sharply.

'Oh yes, Pa had a fantastic job. He used to build robots for Hollywood movies—everything from the robots themselves to animatronic parts for movies like King Kong. It was great. We used to go to LA a lot and hang out at the big studios. You know the movie Terminator 3?'

'Yes.'

'He built half the robots in that. He's a really clever guy.'

Saif tried not to let his excitement show. 'So, he could build a robotic hand?'

'Of course,' smiled Hassan. 'Why do you ask?'

'No reason,' said Saif quickly. 'Just curious.'

'Those were good times,' sighed Hassan. 'But I always wonder what Aunty Ayla must have written to Pa to make him give up his job, put his marriage at risk, and move here, to the middle of nowhere.'

'You never asked?'

'He never told me,' said Hassan. 'In case you haven't noticed, he's not exactly the forthcoming type.'

Saif had to hand it to Aunty Jum Jum; she really knew how to cook. There were cheese sandwiches and *pakoras*, *keema parathas* and *shami* kebabs, and delicious, hot tea.

Taimur pulled his brother aside the minute he saw him. 'I've got lots to tell you,' he whispered.

'So have I,' said Saif. 'We'll talk on the way back.'

'Tuck in, tuck in,' cried Hassan heartily. He was already shovelling a *paratha* in his mouth. Saif smiled. Hassan truly loved life … and food. It showed by the paunch on his tummy. Amina, on the other hand, picked slowly on a *pakora*, and didn't eat anything else.

For an hour they barely spoke, focusing on lunch and on the sound of the river as it rushed past. Amina sat a little apart, painting the Devil's Mouth. From the corner of his eye, Saif could see the canvas. She'd painted fangs, dripping with blood, and evil eyes coming out from inside the cave. Saif looked away, disturbed.

'Well,' said Hassan, pushing a plate of trout bones away from him. 'That was really something. We must do it again tomorrow! But it's getting late; we should make our way back before the light goes.'

As if on cue, Nasir Ali came limping towards them. Saif was startled. He hadn't seen the man approach! Nasir Ali began piling things into the picnic hamper with as much grace as a bull in a china shop.

'Come on,' said Hassan. 'Let's go.'

OXFORD
UNIVERSITY PRESS

'Let's talk later,' whispered Taimur to his brother, as they walked up the cliff steps. 'Privately.'

Saif nodded in agreement. He was amazed to see Taimur holding Amina's hand, helping her up the steeper steps. Whatever Taimur and Amina had talked about, it must have been pretty intense for Taimur to help her like this. His brother didn't often get emotional.

By the time they reached the top of the cliff, Saif was huffing with all his might. And they still had twenty minutes to walk up the hill! Clearly, he and Taimur were very much out of shape for Naran. To pass the time, he began to look around him, enjoying the scenery. On the left, just at the foot of Kimchoo Hill, he saw a little blue bungalow in the middle of some trees. He suddenly remembered what it said in the ghost book. There was a second house, wasn't there, on the hill? Nowhere near as grand, but the only neighbour Kohistan House had for miles.

'Who lives there?' he asked Hassan, panting.

Hassan seemed barely out of breath. 'Oh, that's Mrs Hilary, the Englishwoman.'

'Englishwoman?'

'Yes. She's a widow. She moved here some years ago, after she came for a holiday and fell in love with the place. She loves to climb, too. She and Aunty Ayla used to climb together all the time, in fact. It was a horrible shame. She had the chickenpox when Aunty Ayla wanted to climb up to the Devil's Mouth. Otherwise, she would have been with her.'

'She sounds like an interesting lady,' said Saif.

'Oh she is, she is! Rather grand, actually. Her husband was the Queen's cousin or something. She's terribly proper.'

As if she knew they were talking about her, Mrs Hilary opened the door and waved. 'Yoo-hoo!' she called, smiling. She was a tall, thin, bird-like woman in her mid-forties with short blond hair and sharp green eyes. She wore a safari suit and a beige hunting hat with a leopard print band around it.

'I should warn you both, she's a little eccentric,' whispered Hassan, waving back.

'Oh, you have friends... how jolly. Do come and join me for some tea, won't you?' said Mrs Hilary.

'That's very kind, Mrs Hilary,' said Hassan politely. 'But I'm afraid we must be off home. These are our friends, Saif and Taimur Noon, from Lahore.'

'Noon, you say? Of course, of course. I'm sure I know your grandparents. I do come to Lahore quite often, you know.'

Saif and Taimur smiled politely.

'Are you sure you can't join me for tea? No? Oh, what a bore, what a bore. Perhaps tomorrow then?'

'We'd love to,' said Taimur.

Everyone looked at him, surprised. 'Of course,' said Hassan immediately, not wanting to appear rude. 'What time would be suitable?'

'Oh, we don't stand on ceremony here, come whenever you're free. I say, you chaps haven't seen Sher Khan around have you? Blasted creature escaped again.'

Saif felt slightly panicked. 'Sher Khan? Do you have a lion as a pet?'

Mrs Hilary laughed, in a shrill, bird-like way. 'Good heavens no! What must you be thinking! Sher Khan is actually a python. Oh, no, don't be alarmed boys. He's perfectly harmless, I assure you. I bought him after dear Monty died. One gets a little lonely, up here by oneself.'

'She's also got a dog, a St. Bernard,' said Hassan.

'Oh!' said Taimur, delighted. He loved dogs. 'We used to have one, her name was Beauty. But it got too hot in Lahore to keep her. We should have sent her up here!'

OXFORD
UNIVERSITY PRESS

'Yes, yes, delightful creatures. But I really must find Sher Khan. He has a terrible habit of killing rabbits and leaving their remains on my veranda.'

'I thought pythons swallowed their prey?' asked Saif.

'Oh yes, indeed they do. The rabbits are just for fun. Are you sure you haven't seen him? No? Well, in that case, I look forward to our tea tomorrow, what?'

'Goodbye,' said the twins politely. Saif tried very hard not to burst out laughing.

'Thanks a lot. Taimur,' said Hassan, poking him in the ribs. 'Now why did you have to tell her we'd join her for tea?'

'It seemed a polite thing to do,' replied Taimur. 'Sorry, did I say something wrong?'

Saif shot his brother a look. He knew when Taimur was up to something. ▪

Chapter Nine

A Terrible Accident

That night after their showers, the boys sat by the little fireplace in their bedroom to warm up. Dinner was about to be served, and the electricity had gone again. But they wanted to stay in their room as long as possible, so they could talk about everything they had seen and heard.

As the fire crackled, Taimur told Saif about Amina's mother. 'So she died, because her rope frayed and she fell. It's strange though. Amina says her mother had just bought the climbing rope—that it was brand new.'

Saif looked troubled. 'Well, how could anybody have had anything to do with it? I mean, there were no other ropes or climbing equipment around, and it's impossible to get to the Devil's Mouth without climbing, you said.'

Taimur shrugged. 'Unless someone climbed to the cave before her and cut her rope from above. The person could have pulled up his or her own rope and stayed hidden in the cave until people found Amina's mother, and climbed down later.'

Saif shook his head. 'No, I'm sure someone would have been sent up to check exactly what happened, how she fell. Besides, why on earth would anybody want to kill Amina's mother?'

Taimur sighed. 'I have no idea. But isn't it strange, that both her parents died so suddenly?'

'Yes,' Saif added. 'It is. It's also strange that Aunty Ayla wrote Uncle Hamid a letter that made him rush back here, leaving everything behind in Florida— his career, his wife. And a few months later Aunty Ayla died.'

OXFORD
UNIVERSITY PRESS

'You think he has something to do with it?' asked Taimur.

'I have no idea. I doubt it. We don't even know if she *was* murdered. But we do know that Uncle Hamid is the one who played that nasty joke on us last night, since he used to build robots for a living. Who else would have a robotic hand? We need to figure out why he wants to get rid of us. Maybe we should scout around tomorrow afternoon—oh—no, wait. Thanks to you, we have to go have tea with that Englishwoman—Mrs Hilary.'

'I did that on purpose,' said Taimur. 'I think we should talk to as many people as possible. The more information we have, the better.'

'This is turning out to be quite a mystery,' Saif sighed. 'Maybe we should tell Mama what's going on.'

'You fool! You know the first thing she'll do is send us away. How is that going to help Amina, hmm?'

'You're right Bhai. But tell me, do you still believe in Marcham's ghost?' asked Saif.

Taimur shrugged. 'I really don't know. I think so. I mean, he's been haunting the place for a hundred years, long before Amina's grandparents owned the place …'

'Help! HELP! Somebody HELP!'

Taimur and Saif jumped up in alarm. 'That's Mama's voice,' shouted Saif. 'Come on, quick!'

They ran out of the room, racing through the maze of corridors in the darkness. 'Mama!' shouted Taimur. 'Mama, where are you?'

'Help, get help!'

They followed the sound of Mama's voice and found her crouched by some stairs that led up to the family bedrooms. She was leaning over a body!

'Saif, Taimur, it's Jum Jum. She's fallen down the stairs. I think it's bad. Find some help,' said Mama in a very tense voice.

Aunty Jum Jum lay sprawled on the foot of the stairs. She started to moan. 'Someone pushed me. The ghost. He's going to kill us all.'

'What's happening?' said Uncle Hamid, coming down the stairs slowly. 'I was in my bedroom when I heard the noise. What's going on?'

'Quick,' said Mama. 'It's Jum Jum. She's fallen, and she's delirious. We've got to get her to a hospital. Hamid, you'll come with me?'

OXFORD
UNIVERSITY PRESS

In the darkness, Saif tried to make out Uncle Hamid's face. More than anything, he looked … angry. 'Fine,' he said. 'But I should warn you, we'll be gone overnight. The hospital is too far away to make it back here until the morning.'

'Never mind about that,' said Mama crossly. 'I think she's broken her leg.'

The next few minutes were chaos. Amina and Hassan came rushing out of the dining room. When she saw Aunty Jum Jum, Amina became hysterical. She couldn't stop sobbing and had to be calmed down by Taimur and Hassan. The jeep was prepared for the long journey, with pillows and water and anything else that might be needed on the journey. Worryingly, Aunty Jum Jum had stopped talking. Her face was bright red, covered in sweat, and she was moaning. It took all of Hassan's, Nasir Ali's, and Uncle Hamid's strength to lift her into the jeep. Mama sat with her in the back seat, wiping sweat off her brow with a damp towel.

'Boys,' she said. 'I want you to go straight to your rooms after dinner. Make sure Amina is all right first. With any luck, I'll be back in the morning. Until then, be on your best behaviour.'

'Yes, Mama,' said Saif.

'Yes, Mama,' said Taimur, nodding.

The car sped away down the hill, and Hassan put his arm around Amina, who was still sobbing. 'Come on,' he said, his voice tense. 'We'd better all go and eat something.'

'It's the ghost,' said Amina, in a half-crying, half-gulping voice. 'He's come again. Everyone always dies.'

'She needs to get in bed,' said Taimur. 'She's not going to eat anything in this state. Come on, we'd better go in and make sure she's fine.'

The boys supported Amina, carrying her up the stairs towards her bedroom. In the semi-darkness, Saif, who was trailing behind the others, frowned. Something was fluttering on the side of the banister. 'You guys go ahead,' said Saif. 'I'll catch up in a minute.' He leaned down, searching with his hands.

Amina, exhausted from the crying, fell asleep after about twenty minutes. The boys went downstairs to eat their dinner, now cold. None of them was particularly hungry, and they were all silent during the meal.

'Right,' said Hassan, when they had finished. 'I think it's best we listen to your mother. Let's all go to bed. Things will look better in the morning.'

'Will Aunty Jum Jum be fine, do you think?' asked Taimur.

'Of course,' smiled Hassan. 'She's Aunty Jum Jum. Nothing will keep her down for long!'

The twins wished Hassan goodnight and then went to their room. 'Well, that was exhausting,' said Taimur. 'How horrible. I wonder if the ghost really did do that. Maybe we should get out some of our equipment and see if there are any traces of energy fields around.'

'Don't waste your time,' said Saif. He sounded strangely excited.

'Why? We can't rule out the ghost for sure, can we? I mean, all these odd things are happening.'

'Would a ghost leave this behind?' From behind his back, Saif pulled out a sheet of paper. 'Look, it's a page from an old diary! It must have fallen out of the pocket of the person who pushed Aunty Jum Jum down the stairs!'

'*If* someone pushed her down the stairs. Ok, let me see,' said Taimur, grabbing at the paper. The boys huddled by the fire and started to read.

OXFORD
UNIVERSITY PRESS

The natives are getting restless again. Bunny thinks there will be a mutiny. He's given me the Aagnee Ruby to hide. I must say, it is a frightful burden to bear. But Bunny insists that the ruby cannot stay with him. He's sent his family away, and I agree it's the best thing.

I am doing the same, sending Gertrude and Victor Alexander back to London. My wife and son should not be here at such a tense time. Betty, loyal and faithful as ever, has refused to leave. But I have asked her to go. I am ashamed to say I made promises to her, promises I never intended to keep. Once I am back in England, I shall see that she is properly settled. However, I worry for Bunny's safety, and my own.

The British Raj will not survive any more mutinies. I fear that our time in this part of the world is drawing to a close.

Thank God, I had the presence of mind to build the underground tunnel when Kohistan House was constructed. To my knowledge, nobody besides Bunny and I know that the tunnel even exists. If anything should happen, I shall be safe in the tunnel. It leads to a rather large cave just above the river. I am hiding the Aagnee Ruby there tonight.

I am entrusting this diary to my wife to take it back to England. I shall draw a map of the tunnel, and of where the ruby is hidden, in the cave called the Devil's Mouth.

My dear, if you are reading this, it means I never returned to England to claim this diary. On the next page, you will find a detailed map showing exactly where the ruby is buried. Make sure Bunny and his family know that I guarded it faithfully, until the end. Please take care of Victor Alexander. He is truly loved by his father.

My dearest, I have made many mistakes in my life, and have not always been fair to you. Betty was one of those mistakes. Please forgive me, my darling, because I always loved you, and I always did my duty for Queen and Country. May God have mercy on my soul.

I am, forever, truly yours,

John Marcham, Esq.

In the darkness, Saif and Taimur looked at each other.

'You realize this changes everything,' said Saif.

Taimur nodded. 'Yes. Someone is trying to find the Aagnee Ruby.'

'Whoever it is doesn't know where the entrance to the tunnel is, otherwise they would have found it by now if they had that map.'

Taimur looked at the page once again. 'It has to be Uncle Hamid. Aunty Ayla must have found the diary and written to him about it. He must have rushed over here, hoping to find the ruby for himself.'

Saif looked sceptical. 'And he killed his own sister and brother-in-law to keep them from finding it? That's really hard to believe!'

'Why not? We've seen what a nasty character he is! And look where he was when Aunty Jum Jum fell—right at the top of the stairs, acting as if he only just got there!'

'That's pushing it, Bhai. That's really pushing it. Hassan said Aunty Ayla's death devastated Uncle Hamid. He wouldn't have killed her. And anyway, if *you'd* pushed someone down the stairs, wouldn't you leave the scene of the crime?'

'Then maybe it was an accident. Maybe he only meant to scare her away.'

'And his sister?'

Taimur looked frustrated. 'I don't know … maybe that was an accident too. Maybe he wanted her to see the frayed rope and *think* the ghost was after her so she'd leave the place! I mean, think about it. What could Aunty Ayla have written to Uncle Hamid about—she must have found the diary! She must have told him about the map!'

'Well,' said Saif. 'We know one thing. Amina's parents' deaths were not accidents. Somebody killed them, just like somebody tried to kill Aunty Jum Jum tonight.'

OXFORD
UNIVERSITY PRESS

'Yes,' said Taimur, agreeing. 'Someone wants people to believe in the curse of the Aagnee Ruby, so everyone will leave and they can find the entrance to the tunnel.'

'It means Amina might be next!' cried Saif.

Taimur shook his head grimly. 'Not if we can help it,' he said. 'Come on, let's get some sleep, we have work to do. First thing tomorrow, we have to find the entrance to the tunnel.'

'What are we going to do, find the ruby before anyone else?' asked Saif, incredulous.

In the darkness, Taimur nodded slowly. 'Actually Bhai, that's exactly what we're going to do!' ▪

Chapter Ten

Tea with Mrs Hilary

Early the next morning, Mama called. 'I'm afraid Jum Jum's not doing so well, boys. She's broken her leg in three places, and they have to operate. She's also running a high fever. I have to stay with her because Hamid is insisting that he has to get back to the house!'

Saif and Taimur looked at each other in amazement. Back to the house? What was the rush? Did this mean that Uncle Hamid had found the entrance to the tunnel and was planning to use the map to find the ruby?

'Don't worry boys, I'll be there as soon as I can. Baba's leaving from Lahore tomorrow as well. In the meantime, just behave yourselves. And though Hamid can be … difficult … just listen to what he says.'

Saif and Taimur assured their mother that they would stay out of trouble. But listen to Uncle Hamid! The very person they suspected of hurting Aunty Jum Jum! That they would never do.

Breakfast was a quiet affair. Amina, as usual, did not eating anything. Hassan glared at his father the entire time, and Uncle Hamid had his face behind his newspaper again. He'd only just arrived from the hospital, and when they asked how Aunty Jum Jum was, he snapped, 'She's fine,' before retreating behind the newspaper.

'I thought we could all go trout fishing again, before having tea with Mrs Hilary,' said Hassan to the boys.

Taimur tried to look ill. 'Actually Hassan, neither of us is feeling that well.'

OXFORD
UNIVERSITY PRESS

'What are you talking about?' asked Saif. 'We're perfectly fine … ouch … why did you kick … Oh, I see. I mean … yes, we've both got headaches. And stomach aches. We think we'll stay in this morning, if you don't mind. Maybe do some reading.'

Uncle Hamid put down his paper and stared at them both suspiciously. Saif made his face look pitiful. 'Last night, all the adventure. It really did us both in.'

'Actually, I'm going to my room to sleep,' said Amina.

Hassan looked disappointed, but smiled. 'Well, it's just me then I suppose. I'll take Nasir Ali with me instead. The poor man's looking extremely upset this morning, like he sucked on a bitter lime. You fellows get some rest, OK? We'll meet up after lunch and go to Mrs Hilary's.'

Saif and Taimur were relieved. Now they would have the whole morning to look for the entrance to the tunnel! Uncle Hamid kept giving them strange looks throughout breakfast, but left immediately after, muttering something about moths and hatching. Really, Uncle Hamid had the creepiest hobby. Amina went up to her bedroom, and Hassan left a few minutes later with Nasir Ali. The house was quiet. This was their chance! They crept around as quietly as they could, going from room to room, corridor to corridor, knocking on walls in case there was a hidden entrance. They even crawled into the dark space under the kitchen counter, and came out shrieking when they realized it was full of cockroaches!

A few hours later, Saif and Taimur were back in their bedroom, slumped in exhaustion. 'We've combed every inch of this place,' said Taimur, sighing. 'Nothing! The tunnel is well hidden.'

'This place is a maze. We must have missed something. We'd better try again after Mrs Hilary's tea,' said Saif, pulling a cobweb out of his hair.

'I thought talking to Mrs Hilary would be a good thing, but now I'm regretting it! We could have used the time to find the tunnel,' Taimur sighed. 'Come on, we're covered in dust and dirt and things I don't even want to know about. We'd better get cleaned up.'

'Well, you're the fool who suggested we look up the chimney. Honestly, who's ever heard of a tunnel going up?'

'You didn't have to listen to me,' snorted Taimur.

The boys glared at each other, and started getting ready.

Half an hour later, they came down from their bedroom, wearing formal beige trousers and blue and green shirts. Hassan, who'd come back with several trout and was very pleased with himself, had cleaned himself up. Only Amina looked the same, in her black jeans and black T-shirt. She hadn't even bothered to brush her hair.

'Listen, try to be kind to Amina?' whispered Hassan. 'She really loves Aunty Jum Jum a lot. She's upset and confused.'

The four of them walked down Kimchoo Hill to the pretty little blue bungalow at the bottom. Outside, a massive St Bernard crunched on a bone. He had thick, white fur and a shiny, gold nameplate.

'Wow,' said Taimur, rushing over. He loved dogs.

'He's lovely,' said Saif, joining his brother. The dog wagged his tail and nuzzled up to both of them. He was very friendly.

'Ah, I see you've met Sir Rupert,' said Mrs Hilary, coming out of the bungalow.

'Sir Rupert?' asked Taimur, shaking Mrs Hilary's outstretched hand.

'Yes, named after my father. Sir Rupert Walker.'

Saif shook hands as well, as did Hassan. Amina hung back behind the others.

'Charming, charming. Do come in,' said Mrs Hilary, beaming at all four of them. Today she was wearing dark blue jeans and a crisp, beige shirt, with a red scarf around her thin neck. She also wore thick, green boots that came up to her knees, as well as the safari hat from the day before. She looked like she was going hunting!

'Don't worry about the snake,' she said, ushering them into her house. 'I've taken the liberty of putting Sher Khan back in his cage. I know some of you chaps aren't particularly fond of pythons.'

Taimur sighed with relief. The last thing he wanted was to come face to face with a python!

Inside, the bungalow was very pretty. Mrs Hilary had flowers everywhere, and sunlight beamed through the windows onto yellow walls. The whole place looked so cheerful after the cramped corridors and cobwebs of Kohistan House!

Saif and Taimur wandered around while Mrs Hilary went to prepare tea. One wall of her living room was covered with pictures. Saif went up for a closer look, and whistled. There was Mrs Hilary and her husband, shaking hands with the Queen of England, with the Aga Khan, and standing next to King Fahad of Saudi Arabia. There were several formal pictures taken at balls and in state rooms, where Mr Hilary looked serious in his dinner jacket and Mrs Hilary wore long elegant dresses.

The pictures on the opposite wall showed what an adventurous spirit Mrs Hilary must have. Here she was, skydiving with Princes William and Harry, her hands on both of their shoulders, beaming. In another, she was somewhere in Africa, staring at a giraffe as it ambled by. And in a third, she was climbing a cliff wall, next to Hillary Clinton.

'You sure know a lot of people,' said Taimur, when Mrs Hilary returned, carrying a tray.

'No, don't worry, I can carry it myself, thanks,' said Mrs Hilary. 'Yes, I do know a lot of people. Monty, my husband, was in the Foreign Service. He was an ambassador to several countries during his long years of service to Her Majesty. Really, most people are so charming, once you get to know them.'

'I would think you would be bored, sitting here in Naran, after all this adventure!' said Saif.

'Bored? What nonsense my dear chap! Why, have you done any exploring of the area? There are glaciers to be seen and mountains to be climbed. The adventure is all here, I assure you, boys.'

'We know,' said Taimur, shooting his brother a look.

They sat down for tea, enjoying the smell of baking that was coming from the kitchen. On top of all her adventures, Mrs Hilary baked as well! Taimur felt a pang of homes sickness, remembering how Mama always had chocolate steam pudding or some biscuits waiting for them when they got in from school. He wished Mama were here. She would know what to do.

OXFORD
UNIVERSITY PRESS

Mrs Hilary offered them a currant bun each and some scones with strawberry jam—a proper English tea she said, because there were only so many *samosas* and *pakoras* a person could eat.

Saif, who loved *samosas* and *pakoras*, looked disappointed. But he tucked in nonetheless. As usual, Hassan ate well, and Amina didn't eat a thing.

'How are you, my dear girl?' Mrs Hilary asked, handing Amina a cup of tea. 'Not still brooding, what? Your mother wouldn't have wanted that, you know. Neither would your father. They had adventurous spirits, like me. You must follow in their footsteps.'

Amina looked like she was going to cry.

'It seems from the pictures,' said Taimur quickly, trying to change the topic, 'that you enjoy a lot of sports.'

Mrs Hilary beamed. 'Indeed I do, dear boy, indeed I do! As my Great-aunt Elizabeth always used to say, there is nothing that will cure you as well as fresh air and exercise! It's what I'm always telling Hamid, Hassan's father. But the useless man *insists* on staying inside all day, tending to those moths of his. If it wasn't for Hassan, Amina wouldn't be taken outside at all!'

'I like painting, not sports,' said Amina stubbornly.

'I'm sure you do, dear girl, but a little fresh air never harmed anyone. Why, Great-aunt Elizabeth lived to be a hundred and three years old!'

'I won't live that long anyway,' said Amina. 'The ghost will get me long before then.'

There was a shocked silence. Nobody knew what to say.

Mrs Hilary cleared her throat. 'You know, I keep telling your uncle that Kohistan House is not the place for impressionable young minds, but he doesn't listen. You should sell the place and buy some place smaller and more cheerful. Why don't you talk to him Hassan?'

Hassan scowled. 'It's not like he listens to me.'

'My dear chap, think of Amina.'

'She'll be fine; she's just… it was just a bad night last night, that's all.'

They told Mrs Hilary about Aunty Jum Jum's fall, and she looked dismayed. 'But this is terrible news. With Jum Jum there, at least there was *some* adult guidance. But Hassan, your father is obsessed with his hobby. He spends all day in that dark cellar of his, tending to his moths. He wouldn't know if anything happened to any of you!'

'Cellar?' said Taimur, trying to keep the excitement out of his voice. 'I didn't know there was a cellar.'

Mrs Hilary waved her hand. 'Oh yes, dear boy, a very damp, and a very old cellar. Nobody quite knows why Marcham built the thing, because it was never used. Apparently, Marcham kept the cellar door locked at all times, and nobody was ever let in. It was almost like he was *hiding* something. People accused him of stealing goods from the British Raj, and hiding them there, you know. Quite an unsavoury character. Now, the cellar is being used to hatch moths, of all things!

'Ooooh,' said Saif, clutching his stomach.

'Good gracious dear boy, what on earth is the matter?'

'I'm afraid we're not feeling terribly well,' said Taimur quickly, when his brother winked at him. 'I think we'll have to go home now.'

Mrs Hilary got up quickly, looking alarmed. 'Of course, dear boy, of course! You must leave immediately. I cannot abide sick people. They ruin the health of those around them. Why, I have never had a day illness's in my life! Exercise boys, fresh air! That's what you need! Now go, go. Tell that brute of a servant—what is his name—Nasir Ali, to make you some chicken soup for dinner. Great-aunt Elizabeth swore by chicken soup. It kept her digestive system in order!' ▪

Chapter Eleven

Uncle Hamid's Cellar

Taimur and Saif rushed back to Kohistan House, leaving Amina and Hassan to trail behind them.

'*Array*,' said Hassan, stumbling on a rock, trying to keep up. 'What's the big idea? Wait for us, at least!'

'I'm very sorry,' said Saif, clutching his stomach. 'Feeling very sick. Must get to bed.'

'Yes, and I must help him,' said Taimur.

Hassan shook his head. 'You Lahoris, you're obviously not suited to our climate! Can I get you anything? No, well then go to bed, and I'll ask Nasir Ali to bring you some tea later on.'

The boys raced through the front door towards their bedroom. They ran smack into Uncle Hamid, who was coming down a corridor, rubbing his beard, and looking furtive.

'Watch where you're going,' he snarled.

'We're so sorry, sir,' said Taimur, trying to look innocent.

'What are you doing, running around here like madmen?'

'Actually, we're not feeling very well. We were just on our way to bed,' said Saif. 'In fact, I may throw up very soon.'

Uncle Hamid looked disgusted. 'Well, go then, go. Don't stand around.'

'Thanks, sir,' said Taimur. 'Oh, and sir?'

'What is it now?'

'I was interested to hear about your moth-breeding hobby. It's something I studied at school, actually. I wondered if you'd let me come and see your moths sometime?'

Uncle Hamid looked tense. 'I'm afraid not. It's a delicate time, breeding season. The moths have to be kept in darkness and left undisturbed.'

'Oh, I see. Well, perhaps you could tell me something about them. How often do moths breed?'

'What?'

'I just wondered, is it once a year, or twice a year, or once a week? Is there a particular time of day or night? Actually, while we're on the subject, how many varieties of moths *are* there?'

Uncle Hamid glared. 'It's no business of yours, is it? Watch your step, boy. As if I don't have enough to deal with.'

He stalked down the corridor.

'What was all that about?' asked Saif when they got to their room. 'Why were you asking him all those questions?'

'I just wanted to see how much he really knew about moths, that's all. Didn't it seem like he couldn't answer the questions?'

'Maybe,' said Saif, sighing, lying down on his bed. 'But maybe he just didn't want to. He isn't the friendliest fellow on the planet, is he?'

Taimur frowned. 'But what if the moth thing is just a smokescreen to keep people out of the cellar? What if he's there, looking for the entrance to the tunnel?'

'He would have found it by now, surely. And if he had the map, he'd have found the ruby too.'

'Maybe it's really well hidden,' said Taimur. 'Maybe he hasn't been able to get into the tunnel yet.'

'All I know is, that's an awful lot of maybes,' said Saif yawning. 'You know what? Now I really *am* tired. I'm going to lie down for a while.' He put his head on his pillow and closed his eyes. A little afternoon nap. Perfect.

The next thing he knew was that he was being yanked off the bed and thrown onto the floor.

'What?' he asked crossly, rubbing his shoulder.

'No time for napping now, we've got to get to the cellar!' said Taimur. He was pacing back and forth across the room. 'Baba will be here tomorrow, and he'll take us away. We don't have much time left.'

'We don't even know where the cellar is,' said Saif.

'Yes we do! Uncle Hamid came down the corridor on the left. That leads to the kitchen, remember? There was a locked door in the pantry, but we thought it was a storeroom. That must be the entrance!'

'You're right,' nodded Saif. 'But how do we get inside?'

Taimur sighed. 'I don't know. We'll have to wait until nightfall, when everyone's asleep. Maybe Uncle Hamid leaves the key hanging outside on the wall, or something.'

Saif laughed, shaking his head. 'Do you really think that's likely? I mean, he probably keeps it with him all the time. That's what I would do if I was trying to keep people away from a hidden treasure. The question is, how on earth are we going to get a hold of it?'

'It's pretty easy actually,' said a voice behind them. Both boys jumped and turned around. 'I have a copy. It is, after all, half *my* cellar.' Amina stood at the doorway, her hands on her hips. ■

Chapter Twelve

The Entrance

'Um,' said Saif. 'We were just ...'

'Don't bother,' said Amina, coming into the room. 'Just because I don't talk much, do you think I'm stupid? You guys are up to something, I know it. Tell me.'

'It's better if we don't,' said Taimur gently. 'You might get in trouble. But we need that key.'

'Is it the ghost? Is he coming to kill the rest of us?'

The boys looked at each other. How much should they tell Amina? Was it fair to let her think there was a ghost, after all this? 'Amina,' said Taimur, it's a long story, and I don't think you really ...'

For once, Amina looked fierce, and angry. 'This has something to do with my parents, doesn't it? I've heard you whispering. And don't bother to tell me you're feeling sick—the amount of scones you two ate, there's no way you were ill.'

'I think we should tell her,' said Taimur quietly. 'She deserves to know.'

'Amina, you're ... well, you're delicate. It might upset you a lot,' said Saif, putting his hand on her shoulder.

Amina yanked his arm off and started to yell. 'Oh yes, don't talk to the poor, *strange* little girl in the corner. She's not worth telling anything to. She might fall apart!' Then she started to cry. 'Do either of you know how it feels to lose your parents? Do you? Do you know what it's like, waking up in the middle of the night, *every* night, sweating and shivering at the same time, calling out for your mother? Knowing, deep down, that something *strange* is going on? That something's not right? I need to know why, don't you understand? I need to know why this happened, and who killed my parents.

OXFORD
UNIVERSITY PRESS

Everyone thinks I'm delusional, but I *know* they were murdered. And I've listened to both of you talking when you think you're alone. Have you seen the ghost? Is that it? Did he kill them?'

'It's not the ghost, Amina,' said Taimur quietly. 'Someone did kill them, but it's not the ghost.'

'Then who?' sniffed Amina. 'Why?'

'Come,' said Saif. 'Come and sit by the fire. We have a lot to talk about.'

The boys told Amina everything. They told her about the fake fluorescent hand in the fireplace. They told her about finding the diary page and about the Aagnee Ruby and the tunnel to the Devil's Mouth. They told her their suspicions about Uncle Hamid—that he was trying to scare everyone away. And they told her that they needed the key to the cellar because they had to go down and find the entrance to the tunnel.

'And then somehow we have to find the ruby before anyone else can,' sighed Taimur. 'That way, we can give it back to the Maharajah's family, and whoever is searching for it will give up.'

Amina was strangely calm.

'Are you well?' asked Saif. 'Here, have a tissue. Blow your nose.'

'I'm fine,' she said. 'Actually, I'm more than fine. All this time, I've needed some answers. Now, I feel like I'm starting to get some.'

'It's a lot to take in,' said Saif. 'It must be hard.'

Amina sniffled. 'Actually, it's not, in a funny way. It makes sense. Finally something makes sense. I may not be able to fight a ghost, but I can fight a human being! But you're wrong about one thing.'

'What's that?' asked Taimur.

'It can't be Uncle Hamid.'

'Amina …'

'No,' she said, shaking her head. 'It can't be. He wouldn't murder them. Not for any amount of treasure in the world. He loved my mother.'

'Well how do you explain the hand then? And the fact that he didn't want to answer any questions about moths?' asked Taimur.

'I can't. But I know he's innocent. Besides, if he knew the entrance to the tunnel was in the cellar, he would have found it by now. He shut himself in there months ago.'

'Maybe he's found the entrance,' said Saif. 'Maybe he's just not found the ruby.'

'But he has the map,' said Taimur frowning.

'Maybe the page in the diary with the map is missing, or something. Maybe it fell out, like our page did, and was lost,' said Saif.

'That makes sense,' Taimur agreed. 'You and I are going to have to cover a lot of ground tonight, in that case. Thank God, we brought our torches. We'll go in at midnight, when everyone's asleep. Amina, you can give us the key now.'

'I'm coming with you,' she said.

'Don't be silly,' said Saif. 'It could be dangerous. You must stay in the house.'

'Either you let me come with you, or I'm not giving you the key,' she insisted stubbornly.

Taimur sighed. 'I think Saif's right.'

Amina stood up. She was much smaller than both of them, but the way she was glaring at them was quite fearless. 'Whoever did this killed my mother and, probably, my father too. Whoever did this has tried to scare me out of my wits for the last year. This is *my* battle, not yours.'

Taimur looked at Amina with a new found respect. Somehow, the idea that there was a murderer to be caught had given her strength. 'Very well,' he said at last, 'you can come.'

Saif groaned. 'Bhai …'

'No, its fine,' said Taimur. 'She knows this house inside out. She can make sure the coast is clear.'

'And go in the tunnel when we find it,' Amina insisted.

'And go in the tunnel,' said Taimur wearily, rubbing his temples. He hoped he was making the right decision.

At dinner that night, it was hard to act as if nothing was happening. Hassan kept looking at the three of them strangely and Saif, in particular, found it difficult to keep a straight face. They had decided not to tell Hassan about the cellar. If it *was* Uncle Hamid who was behind the murders, it wouldn't be fair to involve Hassan. His heart would break.

For once, Amina ate properly. In fact, the way she was shovelling roast chicken into her mouth made Uncle Hamid grimace and look at her with distaste. 'Didn't your parents ever teach you any manners?' he growled.

Amina gave him a cold look. 'I'm afraid not. They were too busy dying.'

Nobody knew what to say after that, and dinner didn't last much longer. Mama phoned and told the boys that Aunty Jum Jum was feeling better. 'She's awake, and lucid. But she needs a lot of time to recover. Baba will be with you in the morning. He'll bring you to Mansehra and from here we'll drive Aunty Jum Jum to Islamabad in the jeep. She needs to be in a good hospital.'

'OK Mama,' said Saif, hanging up the phone. 'We're going to have to find the ruby tonight,' he told Taimur. 'It's the only way.'

Taimur nodded. They turned off the lights in their bedroom and pretended to be asleep. It was just as well they did, because sometime later, they heard heavy footsteps approach. Both boys shut their eyes tightly. The door creaked open, and someone stood there for a long time. Then the door started to close, and Saif risked opening his eyes for a quick peep. Nasir Ali was limping out of the room.

'That's interesting, isn't, it, Bhai?' said Saif.

'Very interesting,' replied Taimur, sitting up, supported by his elbows. 'We didn't think of him at all.' Anxiously, they stayed in bed, waiting for midnight to come. Saif yawned once or twice, and Taimur kept poking him in the ribs to make sure he stayed awake. And then it was time. Carefully, they left their bedroom and made their way down the corridor in the dark. They didn't want to use their torches, in case anyone saw them.

When they got to the kitchen, Taimur stumbled and fell and cursed.

'Shhh,' said Saif fiercely.

'Sorry,' Taimur whispered. 'I must have tripped on something.'

'It was my foot, actually,' whispered Amina. 'Took you boys long enough! I've been waiting here for half an hour!'

'We wanted to make sure the coast was clear,' said Saif. 'Come on, we'd better go down into the cellar.'

'No problem,' said Amina, producing a large, iron key. 'Uncle Hamid doesn't even realize that I have this. He thinks that there's only one key, but I found this in Ammi's cupboard, after she died. She must have always had a set.'

They went into the pantry, managed to avoid knocking down several shelves laden with tin cans, and turned the key in the lock on the cellar door. It moaned in protest, and the three of them stood still, petrified that someone would hear them. Amina gritted her teeth, and tried again. This time, the door opened without complaint. 'Thank God,' she said. 'Come on, it's this way.' She led them down some steep stairs to a room that was almost as big as the whole house. 'This is it,' she said.

It was hard to see in the darkness, so the boys turned on their torches. The cellar was damp and mouldy. Water dripped down on one side from a leaky pipe in the corner. On the other side, there were fifty or sixty large glass jars, taking up the whole of the wall. In each jar, a hundred or so moths flew around furiously. The jars looked like they would be heavy to carry.

OXFORD
UNIVERSITY PRESS

'See,' said Amina. 'I told you. Uncle Hamid isn't a murderer. He's obsessed with these moths.'

'Let's look around,' said Taimur. 'The entrance has to be in this cellar, we've looked everywhere else. Knock on the walls to see if they're hollow. Look in every nook and cranny.'

'Not again,' complained Saif. 'I was the one covered in cobwebs the last time, since you made *me* go up the chimney.'

They spread out and began to search. Taimur felt along the walls, while Saif looked under old dusty cloths and bottles. Amina foraged along shelves of paint, brushes, and an assortment of old things left in the cellar because there was nowhere else to put them—an old doll, a pair of roller skates, some Mad Magazines. The only things they didn't touch were Uncle Hamid's moth jars.

After half an hour, they came together again, frustrated. 'No wonder Uncle Hamid didn't find the entrance,' said Taimur, wiping sweaty hair out of his eyes. 'It's impossible.'

Saif started to speak. 'I think we should …'

He was cut off by Amina. 'Look,' she whispered. A bright light was hovering towards them. It looked like the light of a torch, but it was something else entirely, moving up and down and flickering about.

'Quick,' whispered Taimur urgently. 'Everyone hide behind those old sheets. Someone must be coming.'

But nobody came. The light remained. It moved around the glass jars, and hovered there for a while. Then it went out.

Saif felt his arms tingle. 'Another one of Uncle Hamid's tricks?' he asked.

'Maybe it's some sort of remote light that comes on when his moths need it,' said Taimur.

Cautiously, the three of them moved towards the jars.

'Well, I'll be damned,' said Saif, moving his torch across the wall. 'It's another trick,' he said in excitement. 'Look!' He pointed at the jars. Inside, the moths were still moving around in a frenzy. 'Take a really close look,' said Saif. 'You'll see that they aren't moths at all. They're …'

'Robots …' whispered Amina. 'They've got silver electronic lights on the side, see! They must be programmed to go around and around like that.'

'Why on earth would anyone want to pile up jars of robotic moths in a room?' asked Saif, shaking his head in amazement.

Taimur whistled slowly. 'What's the best way to hide an opening or an entrance? How about piling large jars in front of it! Nobody would ever bother to check behind them, would they? I mean, you wouldn't want to deal with all the moths!'

'Why moths though? Why not find something else, or at least use *real* moths and spare yourself the hassle of building robots,' asked Saif, moving his torch across the wall. Taimur shrugged.

Quickly, they all began to move jars. They were not as heavy as they looked. The moth robots were obviously very delicate, because the minute they were jostled, they fell apart at the bottom of the jars.

Almost immediately, Saif spotted a hole in the wall, large enough for a body to crawl through.

'Right,' he said, 'we'll have to go in a single file. I'll lead the way. Amina, you follow me. Taimur will come behind. If anything happens to me, I want the two of you to crawl back and run for help, is that clear?'

Taimur nodded. Amina looked scared, but nodded as well.

'Come on, we've already been here an hour. We've got to find the ruby soon.'

Saif began to crawl, occasionally nicking his elbows on the rock wall. The tunnel led downwards and, luckily, began to open up after a few minutes.

OXFORD
UNIVERSITY PRESS

Saif started to walk, hunched over. After a few minutes, he could walk normally.

Even with their torches, they weren't able to see much. The tunnel was like a large cavern, full of stalagmites and stalactites, with green algae on the walls. They went downwards for at least twenty minutes, and the boys realized they were probably following the slope of Kimchoo Hill.

'We must be under the cliff now,' said Taimur in amazement, looking around. 'We're close to the river. That's why everything is damp. Can you feel the vibration? I can hear it too. Look how silver the rock walls are. It must be from the minerals in the water.'

Amina shivered, and grabbed his hand. They walked on.

Eventually, Saif raised his hand as a signal for them to stop. 'I can see light up ahead. It must be the opening of the cave. We must be at the back of the Devil's Mouth.'

Amina slumped down on a rock, exhausted. 'Now I know how someone was able to kill my mother. They must have followed the tunnel to the entrance where she was climbing.'

'That's also how Governor Marcham must have been murdered,' said Saif. 'Remember the book? The house was entirely locked up, and yet someone managed to kill him.'

Taimur held out his hand to Amina. 'Come on. We're here, in the cave. We've got to start searching. We don't have a lot of time left.'

'For once, my boy, you're correct,' said a voice behind them.

They turned around. There was Uncle Hamid, walking behind them, an ugly gleam in his eyes, and a knife in his hand. He must have followed them! 'Thought you'd snoop around on your own, did you? I knew you were up to something. All that nonsense about stomach aches, all those questions about moths!'

Taimur pushed Amina behind him. 'Run to the entrance. See if you can signal for help.'

Uncle Hamid laughed but his laugh was bitter and strangled. 'Run? Just where are you running to, may I ask? You can't run away from this. None of us can.'

Just then, Saif leaped. He jumped on to Uncle Hamid's back, trying to push him to the floor. 'Help,' he gasped, as Uncle Hamid tried to fling him off. Quickly, Taimur joined his brother, pulling Uncle Hamid down. Uncle Hamid kicked and lashed out, but they knocked the knife to the ground, and together, they managed to pin Uncle Hamid down.

'For a murderer, you're pretty weak,' panted Saif. 'What were you going to do, kill us all? Taimur, grab his leg, will you?'

'Kill you? Kill you?' Uncle Hamid laughed again, maniacally. 'I followed you here to protect you.'

'Nice try,' said Taimur, pushing his knee into Uncle Hamid's stomach. Uncle Hamid gasped.

'Stop it,' yelled Amina. 'Stop hurting him.'

'Hurting him? He was about to kill us,' yelled Taimur back.

'I don't believe that for a second,' shouted Amina. 'You let him go, you hear me?'

Reluctantly, the twins moved away from Uncle Hamid. At least they had the knife now. And there were three of them, and one of him.

Uncle Hamid sat up and rubbed his wrists. 'You boys are pretty strong, you know that?'

'Tell us what's going on, before we change our minds,' snapped Taimur. 'You've known about the Aagnee Ruby all along, haven't you?'

'Yes, since Ayla's letter,' said Uncle Hamid.

'I knew it!' shouted Taimur. 'Didn't I say? He knew there was a treasure to be found and he came here looking for it!'

Amina reached over and took her uncle's hand. 'I know you didn't kill Ammi, Uncle Hamid. Please, tell me what happened.'

'I couldn't save her,' he said, putting his head in his hands. 'I tried, believe me I tried.' Uncle Hamid sighed and started to talk. Ayla had sent him a letter, telling him her life was in danger. Twice, someone had tried to kill the family. Once, the brake cable of their jeep was cut, and they had almost crashed. A second time, a cobra was put in their bedroom in the middle of the night, and only quick thinking saved the day. Ayla was convinced that someone was after the ruby. She'd found Marcham's diary, and read about the Devil's Mouth. But the map was missing—someone had taken it. She was convinced that whoever had stolen the map was trying to get rid of them. First, there were the 'hauntings'. Things would move around, go missing. When that didn't scare them away, the 'accidents' started.

Uncle Hamid shook his head and continued, 'Ayla asked me to come back, to help her find the ruby. I rushed back the very next day, after quitting my job. Sadly, my wife wasn't too happy when I told her why I was coming. She thought it was too dangerous. But I believed that once the ruby was returned to the descendants of the Maharajah, the family would be safe, and I would go back to Miami and pick up my former life. It didn't work out that way, though.'

'What happened to Ammi and Abba?' asked Amina urgently.

'I wish I knew. We'd found the tunnel by then, but had no way to search the entire cave to look for the ruby. It goes back for miles, you know, and splits into different tunnels behind us. It wasn't hard for Marcham to build his tunnel—he just connected it to these other, natural tunnels of the cave. So we had to find a better way of searching. We locked the cellar and I created the moths.'

'It seemed like a very elaborate thing to do, just to keep people from moving jars,' said Saif.

Uncle Hamid shook his head irritably. 'It had nothing to do with that. Watch.' From the pocket of his shalwar kameez, he pulled out one of the little brown objects that looked like a moth. He got up and put it against a wall. The moth crawled up and down and then started to beep.

'What just happened?' asked Taimur.

'Each moth is a laser and sonar scanning system,' explained Uncle Hamid. 'It checks for obstructions in the rock surface up to twenty metres inside. So if there was a ruby hidden in the wall, we'd know about it. Unfortunately, the moths can only scan once, and then they lose power. And they can only scan a small surface at a time.'

'Are you telling us,' said Taimur in amazement, 'that you've been using the moths to search for the Aagnee Ruby?'

'Yes,' said Uncle Hamid miserably. 'It's easier than digging everything up. We just let the moths loose to do their own thing, even though it takes time. Before she died, Ayla and I managed to search the entire floor of this place, miles in each direction, but there was no sign of the Aagnee Ruby. It has to be hidden in one of these walls here, it's the only place left to search. I've already used up hundreds of moths looking, and they take a long time to build.'

'See,' said Amina. 'I told you my uncle was innocent.'

'And brilliant,' said Taimur in admiration. 'I'm sorry, sir. I shouldn't have doubted you.'

'Why not?' laughed Uncle Hamid bitterly. 'I let Amina's parents die. I wasn't able to save them. Ayla got irritated with searching the tunnel, and so she decided to search the cliff wall around the Devil's Mouth instead. Someone must have come here and cut her rope. And Amina's father? The poor man crashed his car, *after* having a heart attack. You know why? Because someone must have poisoned him! He said he thought he knew who killed Ayla, that he just needed proof. He told me he was off to get that proof. Only hours later he was dead, and there was a strange blue tinge on his tongue—arsenic, probably, although the police said there wasn't enough evidence to start a murder inquiry.'

'Oh God,' whispered Amina, putting a hand to her chest. 'Abba'.

'Yes.' Uncle Hamid had tears in his eyes. 'I am responsible. I didn't protect them. Amina, I should have sent you away somewhere safe for your summer holidays. But I wanted you close by. I wanted to be able to keep an eye on the person Ayla loved more than anyone else in the whole world. And yet, how could I leave this place, without bringing the person who killed my family to justice? I swore on your mother's grave that I would punish the person responsible for her and Haroon's death. I swore it and so I put all your lives in danger. And for what? Whoever killed Ayla and Haroon is still running free.'

'You tried to scare us off, didn't you?' asked Saif.

Uncle Hamid nodded miserably. 'Yes. The robotic hand. I thought you'd go running back to Lahore, and that you'd be safe. You didn't believe it was real, though. I realized that the next day when you said nothing about the incident. I'm sorry I was so rude. I was so worried, don't you see?'

'It was brilliantly done though, sir,' said Taimur.

Saif looked at his brother in exasperation. Honestly, all he ever thought about was mechanics! 'What should we do now?' he asked.

Uncle Hamid got up. 'What I should have done a long time ago. I'm sending you boys, and Amina and Hassan away. I'll stay here alone and find the ruby, and Ayla's murderer.'

'I'm not going anywhere,' said Amina.

Uncle Hamid reached down and hugged his niece. 'I am so sorry, *beti*. Can you forgive me?'

'You tried to protect them,' Amina sniffled. 'And I'll always love you for it.'

'Come on,' said Saif. 'Let's go back to the house. It's quite claustrophobic in this tunnel.'

Taimur smiled at his brother. 'You sound like Mrs Hilary. *Get as much fresh air as possible. As my Great-aunt Elizabeth used to say…*' And then he stopped, stunned.

'It's her,' he said.

'What?' asked Uncle Hamid.

'Mrs Hilary.' Taimur looked at the others. 'She's the murderer.'

'Don't be ridiculous,' replied Uncle Hamid. 'She's related to the Queen of England. Her husband left her with millions of pounds. Why on earth would she want to …?'

'Saif, remember Marcham's diary page, the one we found near the stairs when Aunty Jum Jum was pushed! What did he write to his wife? Something about how he'd made mistakes—Betty was one of his mistakes! Betty the maid! She was having an affair with him! And what's Betty short for? *Elizabeth.* Betty the maid is Great-aunt Elizabeth! She must have known about the ruby and told her great-niece, Mrs Hilary!' Taimur spoke so fast that he forgot to breathe, and went red in the face.

'Nonsense,' said Uncle Hamid, shaking his head. 'Mrs Hilary is related to the best people in society. Not to chambermaids and such. Besides, the name could easily be a coincidence. There is more than one Betty in the world, you know.'

'No,' said Saif slowly. 'Taimur is right. Think about it. Mrs Hilary said she couldn't go climbing with Aunty Ayla the day she died because she had the chickenpox. But when we went and had tea with her, what did she say? That she'd never had a day's illness in her life!'

'I don't believe it,' said Uncle Hamid.

'You always were a fool, Hamid,' said a shrill voice from further inside the cave. Mrs Hilary emerged from the shadows, holding a gun. ▪

Chapter Thirteen

Saving Amina

Mrs Hilary pointed her gun directly at them. She sneered. 'Very clever boys, very clever. Got the whole thing sussed, didn't ya?'

Her proper English accent seemed to have disappeared! 'Oh, don't look at me like that fellows. I've always been good at accents, me. Grew up in the East End of London, I did. Lots of different types about, loads of conmen on the take. Easy to learn *a proper English accent, what?*' she mimicked.

'I *thought* that accent was a bit over the top,' said Taimur.

'I don't believe it,' said Uncle Hamid, again, shaking his head. He was obviously in shock.

'No? What don't ya believe, Hamid? That a few false pictures and a funny voice was all it took to convince you that I was a lady? No, don't try to push Amina behind you, Taimur. All of you come here, where I can see you. Good.'

'Your Great-aunt Betty …' said Taimur

'Was a doddering ol' fool,' snapped Mrs Hilary. 'Marcham let her hold the ruby once, you know? She said it was like having her soul ripped out from her body, to have such a priceless gem in her hand and to have to give it up again. Marcham told her he loved her, the ol' codger and married her. But then he sent her away, without as much as a by your leave. He was going to leave her to fend for herself, *and* she was carrying his child. What could she do?'

'So she murdered him,' said Saif.

Mrs Hilary smiled viciously. 'It was no more than he deserved. The idiot told her everything—that there was a tunnel, and that his diary had a map showing where the ruby was buried. Can you believe it? The ol' codger wanted her to protect his wife and son on the way home to England.'

Taimur tried to get his brother's attention. Maybe if they both jumped on her... Very discreetly, Saif shook his head. He knew what his brother was thinking, but a gun was different from a knife!

'But Betty didn't help Marcham's family, did she?' said Saif, trying to distract Mrs Hilary long enough to come up with a plan.

'Course not. Instead, she stole the diary from his wife. She came back to Naran with the diary, climbed up into this cave, followed the tunnel to the house, and murdered Marcham. She fully intended to go back into the tunnel and dig up the ruby after she'd had her revenge. But just then the Rebellion of Jam Git started, and rioters broke into the house. Betty panicked, and

OXFORD
UNIVERSITY PRESS

dropped the diary in her attempt to escape. In the end, she had nothing, no map, and no ruby. There was no way she could come back here—the whole place was on fire, people were being massacred. She barely had enough for a passage back to England. She and her daughter spent years in a poor house in London. Both of them died of consumption. Tragic.'

'So she didn't live to be a hundred and three years old,' said Saif. 'Was anything you told us true?'

'Well, I did have a husband once, that was true enough. But he was a fool and a drunkard. I hit him over the head with a cricket bat and took all his money. It was quite a tidy sum, actually. The fool loved betting on horses. For once, he was lucky.'

'I don't understand,' said Taimur. 'How did you get the map?'

'Before she died, Betty told me all about the diary. So once I stole Frankie—that's my husband's—money, I made my way to Pakistan with a few posh clothes and fake pictures. It didn't take long to befriend Ayla and Haroon,' Mrs Hilary sneered. 'They were the trusting sort. Soon I had the run of the house. The diary was there all along, in the library! The stupid fools didn't know what was under their noses. I only took the map, mind you... the rest was nonsense. Ayla must have found the diary afterwards.'

'So you came here to get the Aagnee Ruby for yourself,' said Saif.

'You got that right, ducky. Trouble is, it's hard to get up 'ere. Unlike you, I didn't have the chance to use the secret entrance. Hamid's good at keeping it all nicely locked up, ain't ya, Hamid? And that Ayla put a right crimp in me plans! It takes an hour to climb up 'ere. Every time I tried, she'd come and join me. Maybe she had her suspicions or something. But she always seemed to *know* when I was coming up 'ere. I could hardly have her following me now, could I? I had to wait, and wait, and wait, until a time when nobody would see me climbing. Otherwise people would put two and two together like. In the end, it was easier to just get rid of 'em, and come up 'ere in me own good time.'

'I swear I'll kill you,' said Uncle Hamid, quietly.

Mrs Hilary laughed shrilly. 'Maybe you will, one day. But for the moment, I'm the one with the gun. I'm also the one with the map. And with the Aagnee Ruby.'

From her pocket, she pulled out the biggest gemstone Saif and Taimur had ever seen. Even in the near darkness, it was dazzling. Mrs Hilary looked triumphant, and dreamy. 'It was hidden in ceiling of the tunnel, can you believe it! None of us thought to look upwards, did we? But it's exactly like Betty described. You can feel the power of it. It's almost like it's alive. It pulsates, like blood in the veins.' She seemed to come back to herself then. 'Too bad you fellows won't have the pleasure of admiring it in more detail.' She put the ruby back into her pocket. Then she threw something at them.

'Here,' she said. 'Climbing rope. Tie yourselves up. Backs together. Nice and tight like. Don't think I won't check. Not the girl. She comes with me, as insurance. I was just about to make my getaway when you got here. This is even better. With the girl as insurance, there's no question of getting caught, and I don't have to risk me neck climbing back down the cliff in the darkness. The girl can show me the way back to the house. That's right, nice and tight, Amina—make sure they can't get free.'

Saif, Taimur, and Uncle Hamid sat with their backs against each other, their arms and bodies tied. Amina tried to loosen the ropes several times, but Mrs Hilary checked them herself, tightened them until Saif and Taimur were wincing in pain, and then nodded, satisfied. 'Come on dearie. We're leaving,'

'Let them go,' shouted Amina, trying to wrestle the gun away. Mrs Hilary narrowed her eyes and gripped Amina's arm. 'I wouldn't make a fuss if I were you, ducky. I might kill your uncle, just for the pleasure of it.'

But Amina was long past hearing. This woman—this evil woman, had killed her parents. Saif and Taimur watched her face as she struggled to pull the gun away. Something had snapped in Amina. She was full of rage.

OXFORD
UNIVERSITY PRESS

'Stop it, I said. You don't believe I'll shoot?' Mrs Hilary wrestled her gun away and then shot Uncle Hamid straight in the knee. Saif and Taimur jumped in shock, Uncle Hamid moaned, and Amina started to cry.

'That's why you should always listen to your Auntie Hettie, girl. That's my real name. Hettie Perkins. Oh stop blubbing—he'll be right as rain, soon enough. I'm off to greener pastures, lads. Maybe I'll buy myself an island or two. I'll let the girl go … eventually … if she behaves. You can stay here and rot for all I care.'

She pulled Amina, shrieking, towards the back of the tunnel that led to Kohistan House. 'Lead the way, dearie. Don't try anything now. You've seen what I can do.'

For a few minutes there was silence, as Saif and Taimur tried desperately to reach Uncle Hamid's knee to staunch the bleeding. Uncle Hamid was pale, and trembling, but said he was all right. Then they heard more gunshots.

Uncle Hamid let out a sob.

'We don't have much time,' shouted Saif. 'We've got to hurry.'

'What do you suggest we do?' Taimur snapped.

'Cut the ropes,' said Saif. 'If I can just reach … got it!'

'What are you doing?'

'Uncle Hamid's knife! It was in my pocket the whole time! If I pass it to you, do you think you can get a hold of it? I can't get a proper grip.'

After a moment of fumbling, Taimur had the knife in his hands, and started to cut ropes. With his hands tied behind his back it was difficult work. He started to sweat and strain. Eventually though, they were free!

'Come on,' said Saif. They tore off a piece of Uncle Hamid's shirt, and used it to stop the bleeding.

'I'll be alright,' grunted Uncle Hamid, gritting his teeth in pain. 'It's a clean wound. Now, for God's sake, go after them. I'll follow at a slow pace. But we've got to get Amina!'

Saif hesitated, and then nodded. The two of them went racing down the tunnel. Almost immediately, they came to an abrupt halt. The tunnel was blocked!

'The gun,' cried Uncle Hamid, limping from behind. 'The walls in the tunnel are old, and badly supported. She must have used the gunshots to cause an avalanche of rocks. She's blocked our way!'

'We've got to climb down the front of the cave then,' said Taimur. 'Come on, to the entrance!'

They raced back the way they came. Mrs Hilary's climbing equipment, her ropes and grapple hooks, were still there. Saif and Taimur looked at Uncle Hamid. Saif shook his head. 'There's no way you'll manage this. I'm not even sure *we'll* manage this.'

'I have faith in you boys,' said Uncle Hamid. He was sweating profusely, and looked like he was about to pass out. 'First find help and get to Amina. Then come back here for me. Amina first though, you understand? Oh, stop looking at me like that. I told you, it's a clean wound. I won't bleed to death.'

Saif nodded, and started to organize the equipment. Taimur pulled him aside. 'How are we going to do this, Bhai? Neither of us has ever climbed down a cliff wall before.'

'We'll manage somehow,' said Saif. They looked at each other for a long time, both of them scared. Then they hugged each other tightly. Whatever happened, they would be together.

Mrs Hilary had left the climbing rope and grapples attached to the cliff wall, which made it easier. They'd never be able to figure out the grapples—that was for certain.

OXFORD
UNIVERSITY PRESS

'Boys?' said Uncle Hamid.

'Yes?'

'Try not to dawdle, will you?' He smiled painfully at them.

Saif and Taimur smiled back, and then took deep breaths. They tied themselves to the climbing rope, so that if one of them slipped and fell, the other could support him. Saif went down first, and then Taimur.

The first thing they noticed was the cold. The cliff wall was almost a hundred feet high, and the wind was fierce. Their hands became numb, their ears burned from the wind. Still, they climbed down, as carefully as they could. 'Look for natural holes in the cliff,' shouted Saif to his brother. 'See where my hands are? Just be careful.'

From above, Taimur nodded. There was no way he was going to look down. He followed Saif as best he could. It seemed like hours went by, as he moved his legs from one natural foothold to another. His arms burnt from the effort, and his legs felt like they were on fire. The rope swayed with the wind, making it even harder to get a grip. At one point, Taimur lost his footing and panicked, hanging to the rope for dear life.

'Keep calm, Bhai,' shouted Saif from below. 'You can do this! Just pretend this is a football game. Close your eyes. Concentrate on getting to the ground!'

Eventually, Taimur managed to stick his foot onto a jutting rock, and both boys exhaled slowly. That was a close one. They kept on going, thinking about Amina, and what might happen to her if they didn't make it down. They thought about Uncle Hamid, and the fact that he would bleed to death if nobody rescued him. Mostly, they thought about Mama and Baba, and how much they missed them.

Finally, just when they thought they couldn't bear it anymore, they were at the bottom. Neither boy felt the cold anymore. They were drenched in sweat. Saif gave his brother a beaming smile. 'We did it Bhai! We actually did it! I thought we were goners for sure!'

Taimur smiled back weakly. 'Come on. We've got to keep moving. Where do you think Mrs Hilary's taken her?'

'One of us should go to the bungalow. She may have gone there to get some of her things. The other should go to the house in case she's still in the tunnel, and also to get some help,' said Saif.

Taimur looked strained. 'There's a slight problem. We're on the wrong side of the river for the stairs!'

Saif groaned. It was true. The river rushed furiously past, and the rough stone stairs were on the other side of it, tantalizingly close. Saif sighed. 'We'll just have to wade our way through. Don't worry. I went in with Hassan the other day, and it's really not that deep. At this time of night, we'll freeze though. The water is icy—it's melt from the glaciers.'

There was nothing else for it. 'Let's go,' said Taimur.

They swam as best as they could. At one point, the rushing water came up to their necks and jostled them around. The brothers held on tightly to each other, supporting one another when one slipped on a slimy rock or gulped too much water. Somehow, they made it to the other side and crawled their way to the stairs. By the time they finally reached Kimchoo Hill, they were shivering violently, and near exhaustion.

'We've got to keep going, Bhai. We've got to get help,' said Taimur.

'I know,' replied Saif. 'Believe me, I know. Let's both go to the bungalow. I don't think either of us should go anywhere alone when we're in this state.'

Taimur nodded.

The first thing they noticed was that all the lights were on. The boys crept up to the front window as quietly as they could. There was Amina, tied to a chair, looking forlorn.

'Careful,' said Saif, putting a hand out when his brother tried to rush in. 'She could still be in there.'

'We've got to take a chance,' said Taimur. 'If only there was something we could use. Some sort of weapon. We shouldn't have left the knife with Uncle Hamid.'

'He needed it more than us,' whispered Saif.

They opened the front door cautiously, and crept in as quietly as they could.

Amina noticed them immediately, her eyes widening. She moved her head towards the kitchen, so the boys would know Mrs Hilary was still in the house. They nodded and started to untie her, moving as fast as they could, praying they wouldn't be discovered.

'I can't believe it. How can the car choose a time like this to stall?' Mrs Hilary muttered from inside the kitchen. 'Well dearie, it looks like we'll have to go up to the house and steal your jeep, eh?'

And just when Saif and Taimur untied the last of the ropes binding Amina, Mrs Hilary walked into the living room.

Her eyes narrowed. 'Well, well, I wasn't expecting you to be that fast. Just as well. I can finish the job properly this time.' She lifted up her gun.

Saif and Taimur pushed Amina out the front door. They stood side by side; facing Mrs Hilary. They looked at each other, too emotional, and too exhausted to speak. Mrs Hilary smiled and aimed.

The twins closed their eyes. A shot rang out.

All Taimur knew when he opened his eyes was that he was still standing. Oh God, Saif! He looked at his brother, and was relieved to see that he too was in one piece, although swaying slightly, as if in shock.

And then they looked at Mrs Hilary. She lay crumbled on the floor, the gun still in her hands. Behind her stood Nasir Ali, holding a rifle. Standing right next to him was Baba.

It was a strange thing. For a moment, Taimur felt like he was floating. There was Baba, coming towards them, saying something, but Taimur couldn't make out the words. Everything was muffled. Everything seemed like it was coming from underwater. And then everything went black. ∎

Chapter Fourteen

Nasir Ali's Secret

When Taimur opened his eyes, he found himself lying in a bed. His mouth was dry, and every inch of him ached. He groaned.

'Awake at last, are we?' said a jolly voice. It was Hassan. He was standing over him, beaming.

'Your father ... Amina ... Saif,' croaked Taimur, trying to get up.

Hassan put his hand on Taimur's shoulder. 'Relax. Everyone is fine. You're in a hospital in Islamabad. You've been asleep for two full days.'

'It feels like it too,' groaned Taimur. 'The others? Are they here?'

Hassan nodded his head towards the bed next to Taimur's. 'If you can crane your neck, you'll see your brother is sound asleep. He didn't last much longer than you, as a matter of fact. Keeled over after making sure you were okay. The doctors want to keep both of you under observation for a couple of days. You've both got a touch of bronchitis, which, after your little river swim, is hardly surprising.'

Taimur lay back, exhausted, his chest hurting. 'What happened?'

'What happened was that you two went on an adventure without me,' said Hassan, pouting. 'Hardly fair, after I taught you how to fish, I mean, there was buried treasure and everything!'

Taimur sighed. 'I'm sorry. We just ... we were afraid that your father ...'

Hassan smiled. 'Don't worry, I know. When they carried Papa back through the tunnel, he was covered in blood. It took ages too, removing all those rocks! I thought I was going to have a heart attack. I realized how much I really love him. I have you and Saif to thank for saving his life.'

'Hassan, your father …' Taimur began.

Hassan sighed. 'He told me the truth about how he came here to protect Aunty Ayla. My mother knew all about Aunty Ayla's 'accidents'. She should have respected that Papa wanted to protect his sister. It's funny you know. For ages, I've been blaming him when my mother is also responsible for what happened between them.'

'Do you think they'll get back together now?' asked Taimur.

Hassan shrugged. 'They're talking. She's flying over. Who knows?'

'Maybe your father will move back to Miami, now that the murderer has been found.'

'I doubt it,' replied Hassan. 'He wants to stay in Pakistan for Amina's sake. She needs all the stability she can get.'

'Is it all over then?' said a voice from the corner.

Taimur turned his head.

Hassan smiled. 'Saif, my friend, you're awake at last.'

'I've been listening to you two nattering on for quite some time,' said Saif grumpily. 'Honestly, what's a person to do to get some sleep around here?'

Taimur leaped out of bed, all this exhaustion forgotten. He jumped on his brother.

'Ouch,' cried Saif. But he was smiling widely.

'When you two have quite finished, there's an awful lot of people who want to speak to you,' said Hassan.

Saif looked up. 'What happened to Mrs Hilary? Is she dead? Hettie Perkins or whatever her name is?'

Hassan shook his head. 'She was shot in the shoulder. She's recovering. The police have already arrested her, although she's insisting it was all a misunderstanding, and that she is in fact related to the Queen.'

'Ah good, you're awake,' said a voice from the doorway. Baba walked in, with Amina trailing shyly behind.

The twins jumped on their father, and he laughed heartily. 'The minute I turn my back, the two of you get into trouble! Thank God I drove so fast and got to Naran when I did!'

Both boys felt their hearts light up. Now that Baba was here, they knew everything would be fine.

'How did you find us, Baba?'

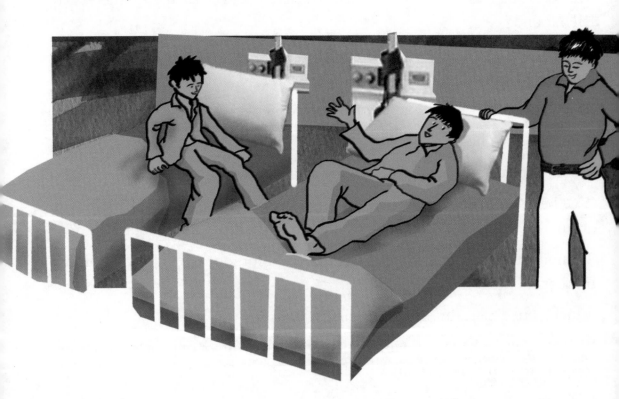

OXFORD
UNIVERSITY PRESS

Baba sat down on Saif's bed in between the boys. He looked so happy to see them. 'Well, I decided to drive straight through the night, even though it meant getting to the house at an ungodly hour and disturbing our hosts. I didn't like the idea of you boys being alone—*not* because I felt you were in danger, but because your hosts might have a nervous breakdown, left all alone with you two devils!'

Saif and Taimur giggled. From the doorway, Amina smiled.

Baba's smile vanished. 'Nasir Ali let me in, but when you weren't in your beds, he panicked and, obviously, I was hysterical. We searched all through the house, and then Nasir Ali took me to Mrs Hilary's. He told me that he thought your lives were in danger and that someone was trying to kill you. Can you imagine what that did to my blood pressure?'

'Nasir Ali knew that all along?' asked Saif, amazed.

Baba nodded his head. 'Oh, yes. He may look like a brute, but he's quite an interesting fellow. Nasir Ali even had his suspicions that Mrs Hilary was the one who was after the ruby. But he had no proof. He spent most of his time in the tunnel, trying to find the ruby himself.'

'He knew about that too?' asked Taimur.

'Where's the ruby now?' asked Saif, interrupting.

Baba laughed. 'So many questions! Actually, the ruby is with Nasir Ali.'

'What!' exclaimed both boys.

'Why?' shouted Saif. 'It should go to …'

'To the descendents of the Maharajah Duleep Bargoza, who are its rightful owners,' said Baba.

Taimur nodded. 'Exactly.'

'Would you believe that Nasir Ali's family has worked for the Maharajah's descendents for seven generations? He was entrusted with finding the Aagnee

Ruby and protecting the Maharajah's heirs, just like his father before him, and his father's father before that.'

'So Nasir Ali will take the ruby to them?'

'Oh yes,' said Baba, winking. 'Better than getting all bureaucratic about these things, don't you think? If anyone else got involved there would be a lot of red tape, a lot of *tamasha* about jurisdictions, and all that. I understand that the Maharajah's great-grandson is a boy with a lot of potential, but he lives in near poverty. It was horrible what happened to the family after the rebellion. They were thrown out of their home, stripped of all their possessions, and nobody wanted anything to do with them.'

Baba put an arm around both boys. 'The family believes the Aagnee Ruby is its lifeline—its lucky charm. Maybe now they will have some good fortune. Besides, Nasir Ali's so happy to have fulfilled his responsibilities, he is almost smiling! Now that he has nothing else to do, I offered him a job at Nurpur,' Baba smiled mischievously.

'I think I'd prefer him to stay with us, Uncle Adnan,' said Amina. She came towards the bed. 'He is, after all, part of the only family I have left.'

Taimur blinked. Amina was not wearing black! In fact, she was wearing a crisp white shalwar kameez with little roses on it, and had brushed her hair. She looked …. not happy exactly, but calm. Calm and relieved. Hassan hugged her, and she smiled at the twins. 'I don't know how to thank you,' she said quietly.

The boys blushed, embarrassed. Luckily though, they didn't have to reply, because they were suddenly lifted off the ground and into a heaving bosom that smelled strangely like Amla hair oil.

'Oh boys,' Aunty Jum Jum gushed. 'What *heroes* you are, saving my Hamid and my Amina. I could just *squeeze* you forever!' The boys laughed, and Saif was surprised to realize he'd *missed* Aunty Jum Jum!

It was a funny sight. Aunty Jum Jum's left leg was in a cast, and she hobbled around on crutches. Uncle Hamid came in and stood next to her, his right leg also bandaged up. The pair of them, one short and large, and the other tall and thin, both on crutches, was quite funny to see! What was more shocking was when Uncle Hamid came up and hugged them both!

'You're good boys,' he muttered, embarrassed at the display of emotion.

And then suddenly there was Mama too, holding them both as tightly as she could, and crying. 'The minute you're feeling better, I'm going to kill you both,' she said, sniffling.

After that, there was a little party in the room. Mama had brought cakes and biscuits, and everyone sat around to chat and eat.

Amina sat next to Taimur and Saif. 'Maybe you'll come back to Kohistan House with me when you're feeling better? It's all going to be so different now. We'll have a lot of fun.'

'I wish we could,' said Taimur. 'But we have to get back to Lahore. Our cousin, Smooch, spends one month of every summer there with us, and he's arriving in a few days.'

'But you can come and join us in Lahore!' said Saif. 'We'll have great fun— and we can play football, go swimming, and watch films. We'll even do some painting, what do you think?'

Amina's face lit up. 'I'd love that! I don't … well, I don't have many friends.'

The boys smiled. 'What about us? We're your friends!' said Taimur.

'Yes,' said Saif wryly. 'I mean, it's not everyday that you go through an adventure like we did! And you were very brave, taking on Mrs Hilary and trying to steal her gun.'

'Can I go to Lahore Uncle Hamid?' asked Amina, pleading.

Uncle Hamid's eyes twinkled. 'Of course! We should *all* go. It's about time we left that cursed house and did something as a family.'

'It's not really cursed though, is it?' said Saif. 'I mean all that malarkey about the ghost. It all turned out to be you, trying to keep people away, and Mrs Hilary, trying to cause accidents.'

Uncle Hamid shrugged. 'I suppose so.'

Taimur looked at him. 'Actually sir, I've been meaning to ask you a question. The sonar/laser moth devices were in jars in the cellar, and we never thought of looking there for the entrance to the tunnel. The only reason we did was because there was a light that came and hovered around them. Was that some sort of energy or battery device?'

Uncle Hamid looked blank. 'I have no idea what you're talking about.'

'You know, the light,' said Saif.

'No, there was no light. The moths' batteries are self contained. Maybe you imagined it.'

Saif, Taimur, and Amina all looked at each other. 'Could it be?' asked Taimur.

'The ghost …' whispered Amina. 'He helped us.'

'But I'm not sure there really was a ghost,' said Saif.

'Maybe not, Bhai, but I do know one thing,' said Taimur, munching happily on a chocolate biscuit.

'What's that?'

'Next summer, if Amina will invite us back, we'll find out for certain! And we won't leave until we have our answer!'

The three of them burst out laughing. ▪

OXFORD
UNIVERSITY PRESS

Glossary

Pg 1 shudder	tremble
Pg 1 waddled	to walk with short steps in a clumsy swaying motion
Pg 4 rickety	likely to collapse e.g. a rickety wooden table
Pg 4 ghouls	evil spirits that rob graves and feed on the flesh of dead bodies
Pg 4 infrared	rays having a wavelength just greater than that of the red light at the end of the visible range
Pg 4 foregoing	going without (something desirable); giving up
Pg 5 resignation	acceptance of something undesirable but inevitable
Pg 5 tardiness	delaying or delayed beyond the right or expected time
Pg 5 outstretched	extend or stretch out
Pg 6 dissuaded	to talk someone out of a plan or course
Pg 7 angelic	exceptionally beautiful, innocent, or kind
Pg 7 spitting image	exact copy
Pg 7 grimaced	frowned; made an unpleasant face
Pg 7 knack	a special skill or ability that you have naturally
Pg 7 antics	foolish, outrageous, or amusing behaviour
Pg 7 mousy	timid
Pg 7 darting	moving suddenly and rapidly
Pg 8 intimidated	feeling frightened
Pg 8 battleaxe	an aggressive older woman
Pg 8 disheartened	disappointed
Pg 8 disdain	dislike; consider inferior
Pg 8 sturdy	strongly and solidly built or made
Pg 8 discontented	unhappy
Pg 8 contemptuously	the feeling that a person or a thing is worthless or beneath consideration

Pg 9 huffily	being easily offended or showing annoyance
Pg 9 paranormal	events or phenomena beyond the scope of normal scientific understanding
Pg 9 decapitated	with the head cut off
Pg 10 palpitation	a rapid heartbeat due to fear, anxiety, illness, etc.
Pg 10 disconcerting	disturbing
Pg 11 snort	a noisy sound made by breathing forcefully through the nostrils, as a horse does
Pg 12 scrambling	moving quickly and awkwardly, by using one's hands as well as one's feet
Pg 12 beaming	radiant
Pg 13 inscrutable	impossible to understand
Pg 14 plagued	annoyed; bothered
Pg 14 cronies	close friends (meant in a disapproving way)
Pg 14 rebellion	an armed resistance to change government or ruler
Pg 15 literally	exactly
Pg 15 lifeblood	driving force
Pg 15 gouged	cut out
Pg 15 mystic	having spiritual powers or qualities that are difficult to understand or to explain
Pg 17 deadpan	expressionless
Pg 17 caving in	falling in towards the centre
Pg 17 barrelled	moved very fast
Pg 17 cooped up	kept in a small cramped space
Pg 17 ghastly	terrible
Pg 17 bookish	interested in reading and studying, rather than in more active or practical things
Pg 18 meek	quiet, gentle, and always ready to please others without expressing one's own opinion
Pg 18 secluded	private, removed from public view

OXFORD
UNIVERSITY PRESS

Pg 18 glaciers	huge masses of ice slowly flowing and compacted snow down the mountains
Pg 19 electromagnetic	operating on both electrical and magnetic fields
Pg 19 whatsits	persons or things whose names one cannot recall, does not know, or does not wish to specify
Pg 19 sulked	was in a bad mood; became angry and upset
Pg 19 to cast	to throw the hooked and baited end of a fishing line out into the water
Pg 19 amateur	non-professional
Pg 20 formidable	inspiring fear or respect through being impressively large, powerful or capable
Pg 20 maneuvering	a series of physical moves requiring skill and care
Pg 21 craned	leaned or stretched over something in order to see something better
Pg 21 levelled off	brought to an even level
Pg 22 turrets	small towers on top of a wall or building, especially a castle
Pg 22 yanked	pulled with a jerk
Pg 22 mutilated	badly damaged
Pg 22 deformed	having an abnormal shape because of wrong growth
Pg 22 malevolently	having or showing a desire to harm other people
Pg 24 to make do with	to manage with whatever is available
Pg 26 fluorescent	brilliant, brightly coloured, visible in the dark
Pg 26 sinister	suggesting or threatening evil
Pg 26 conned	tricked into doing or believing something
Pg 27 sludge	thick, soft, wet mud or a similar substance
Pg 29 idolized	admired
Pg 29 goatee	a small, pointed beard on a man's chin
Pg 29 patrician	aristocrat, or nobleman
Pg 30 hysterically	in a wildly uncontrolled way
Pg 30 prod	to poke with a finger, or pointed object

Pg 30 snarled	to say something in anger, to lash out
Pg 31 kitted out	provided with appropriate clothing or equipment
Pg 31 ruffling	making or becoming disarranged; upsetting
Pg 33 tackle	the equipment used for a particular sport or activity, e.g. fishing
Pg 35 inaccessible	unreachable, out of reach
Pg 35 pulleys	a set of wheels over which a rope or chain is pulled in order to lift or lower heavy objects
Pg 35 cable car	a car drawn by a moving cable, as across a canyon, up a steeply inclined street
Pg 35 feisty	aggressive, energetic
Pg 36 frothing	bubbling; a mass of small bubbles in liquid
Pg 36 tugged	pulled (something) hard or suddenly
Pg 36 waded ... in	moved through shallow water
Pg 36 crestfallen	sad and disappointed
Pg 37 accumulated	collected or gathered together a number or quantity of something
Pg 37 burly	a large and strong man
Pg 37 squint	to look at something with partly closed eyes to keep out bright light or to see better
Pg 38 jutting	sticking out
Pg 39 dwelling	to think or talk about something, to look at something for a long time
Pg 41 haunches	the lower part of the body below the hips, i.e. in a human or animal
Pg 42 grimly	looking or sounding very serious and unhappy
Pg 43 animatronics	the technique of making and operating lifelike robots, especially for use in films
Pg 44 forthcoming	about to happen or appear
Pg 46 eccentric	odd; unconventional
Pg 48 frayed	unravelled or worn at the edge

 OXFORD
UNIVERSITY PRESS

Pg 50 sprawled	to lie or fall with limbs spread awkwardly
Pg 50 delirious	in an excited state and not being able to think or speak clearly
Pg 52 banister	the supports and handrail of a staircase
Pg 53 mutiny	an open rebellion against authority, especially by soldiers or sailors against their officers
Pg 54 sceptical	doubtful; unconvinced;
Pg 55 incredulous	unwilling or unable to believe something
Pg 60 ambled by	walked past or moved at a leisurely pace
Pg 60 ambassador	a high ranking diplomat sent by a state as its representative in a foreign country
Pg 61 brooding	thinking deeply about something; appear threatening
Pg 61 impressionable	easily influenced
Pg 61 scowled	frowned; expressed displeasure or anger
Pg 62 dismayed	worried and sad; disappointed
Pg 62 unsavoury	objectionable; unpleasant
Pg 63 furtive	secretive; stealthy
Pg 64 smokescreen	action carried out to hide what one is really doing or intending
Pg 66 pantry	a small room or cupboard in the kitchen, in which food, crockery, and cutlery are kept
Pg 69 delusional	deceiving or making oneself believe something that is not true
Pg 71 lucid	clear; easy to understand; showing an ability to think clearly
Pg 72 gritted	clenched (the teeth) especially in order to keep one's resolve
Pg 73 nook and cranny	everywhere
Pg 73 foraged	searched widely
Pg 73 tingle	to have a prickling, stinging sensation e.g. due to excitement
Pg 74 frenzy	uncontrolled excitement or wild behaviour

Pg 74 nicking	making a small cut or notch
Pg 75 cavern	a large cave
Pg 75 stalagmite	cone-shaped mineral deposit on cave floors formed by dripping water
Pg 75 stalactite	an icicle-shaped mineral deposit that hangs from the roof of a cave and is formed by dripping water
Pg 75 algae	very simple plants with no real leaves, stems or roots that grow in or near water
Pg 78 obstruction	a hindrance, something that stops you going further
Pg 79 arsenic	a silvery-white, brittle poison
Pg 79 exasperation	extreme annoyance especially if one cannot do anything to improve the situation
Pg 80 claustrophobic	causing discomfort or fear in confined or cramped places
Pg 81 sussed	discovered; figured out
Pg 81 doddering	slow and unsteady
Pg 81 codger	an elderly man
Pg 81 fend	look after and provide for oneself
Pg 83 massacre	brutal slaughter of people
Pg 83 consumption	a wasting disease, especially tuberculosis
Pg 83 crimp	to have a bad or negative effect on something
Pg 84 pulsates	beat or throb in a rhythm
Pg 84 wincing	the facial expression due to pain, or distress
Pg 85 blubbing	sobbing or crying noisily and uncontrollably
Pg 85 to staunch	to stop the flow of blood
Pg 85 fumble	to express oneself or deal with something clumsily or nervously
Pg 86 grunted	made a low, inarticulate sound to express effort
Pg 86 profusely	produced in large amounts
Pg 86 grapples	iron hooks attached to ropes, used in climbing and also to drag in boats

OXFORD
UNIVERSITY PRESS

Pg 87 to dawdle	to move slowly, to take a long time to do something
Pg 87 swayed	moved slowly from side to side
Pg 88 tantalizingly	attracting one towards something out of reach; tempting
Pg 88 forlorn	pitifully sad and lonely
Pg 89 to stall	to stop suddenly because of a lack of power or speed
Pg 89 muffled	sound reduced by covering up its source
Pg 90 croaked	spoke with a low hoarse voice; muttered discontentedly; grumbled
Pg 90 bronchitis	a respiratory chest infection
Pg 91 shrugged	raised one's shoulders and then dropped them to show that one did not know or care about something
Pg 93 ungodly	outrageous
Pg 93 brute	cruel or insensitive person
Pg 94 jurisdiction	area under certain and specific legal control
Pg 94 bureaucratic	concerned with a lot of paperwork, and excessive correctness in procedure
Pg 94 red tape	official rules that seem more complicated
Pg 96 malarkey	nonsense

Book **Piracy** and **Plagiarism** are **Crimes**. Beware of both!

Look out for the new security label whenever you purchase an Oxford textbook or supplementary reader. Labels with the features shown below are proof of genuine Oxford books.

- An iridescent circle with an image of the Quaid's mausoleum changes colour from orange to green when viewed from different angles.

- The labels tear if peeled from the book cover.

- The labels have security cut marks on the right and the left side to prevent them from being peeled off and reused.

- The word 'ORIGINAL' appears when the area beside 'SCRATCH HERE' is rubbed with a coin.

- The words 'OXFORD UNIVERSITY PRESS' written in very small print become visible when viewed under a magnifying glass.

Do not accept the book if the label is missing, has been torn or tampered with, the colour on the security label does not change, or the word ORIGINAL does not appear upon rubbing the area with a coin.

Pirated books can be recognized by:

- inferior production quality
- low-grade paper
- variations in texture and colour
- poor print quality
- blurred text and images
- poor binding and trimming
- substandard appearance of the book

OXFORD
UNIVERSITY PRESS

If you suspect that you are being sold a pirated book without the security label, please contact:

Oxford University Press, No. 38, Sector 15, Korangi Industrial Area, Karachi-74900, Pakistan.
Tel.: (92-21) 35071580-86 • Fax: (92-21) 35055071-72 • Email: central.marketing.pk@oup.com
Website: www.oup.com/pk • Find us on